The Amish Veronica Series #2

You Have Ravished My Heart

With blessings!
Stephanie

Stephanie Schwartz

YOU HAVE RAVISHED MY HEART

Copyright © 2024 by Stephanie Schwartz

ISBN: 979-8-88653-293-7

Published by Satin Romance
An Imprint of Melange Books, LLC
White Bear Lake, MN 55110
www.satinromance.com

The King James Bible Version is used throughout.

Permission has been granted by the editor, Milo G. Miller, of *The Budget* to quote sections of it.

Permission has been granted to include information about Humpback Dairies in Miller, Missouri by Sam Hochstetler, owner.

Permission to quote Catherine Doherty's writings has been granted by Madonna House Publications, Combermere, Ontario, Canada.

Names, characters, places, and incidents depicted in this book are products of the author's imagination or are used fictitiously. Any resemblance to actual events, locales, organizations, or persons, living or dead, is entirely coincidental and beyond the intent of the author or the publisher. No part of this book may be reproduced or transmitted in any form or by any means, electronic or mechanical, including photocopying, recording, or by any information storage and retrieval system, without permission in writing from the publisher except for the use of brief quotations in a book review or scholarly journal.

Published in the United States of America.

Cover Design by Caroline Andrus

Contents

Author Note: v
*The Glossary** xi

PART ONE
1. From Afar — 3
2. My Cup Runneth Over — 9
3. The Way of the World — 17
4. Crackers — 22
5. Peppa Pig — 29
6. Flying Squirrels — 37
7. Multi-tasking — 42
8. Waernt iss Mamm? — 49
9. Zebras — 57
10. A Mail Order Bride — 63
11. No Rest For The Wicked — 69
12. Blowing Raspberries — 83

PART TWO
13. Rhinoceros and Elephants — 91
14. Plastic Daisies — 96
15. Plum Ferhoodled — 104
16. A Horse Named Rapunzel — 113
17. The Holy Toast and Yummasetti — 119
18. Barn Raising — 124
19. Playing On The Outhouse Roof — 131
20. Flat Squirrels — 137
21. Macaroni and Cheese — 141
22. To Have and to Hold — 145
23. Fugitives — 148

PART THREE

24. Fruit Loops For Pigs — 159
25. Mamm is Back — 164
26. Stranger Danger — 169
27. Lollipops and Roses — 172
28. Out of the Mouths of Babes — 183
29. No Fair! — 187
30. Blastoff — 192
31. The Amish Wedding Wagon and Dirt Pudding — 198
32. Watching The Radio* — 203
33. Cloudy With a Chance of Meat Balls — 208
34. The Wedding — 214
35. Purple Eggs — 218
36. Worry Ends — 224

MERRY AMISH CHRISTMAS

Chapter 1 — 231

Acknowledgments — 241
Thank You For Reading — 243
About the Author — 245
Also by Stephanie Schwartz — 247

Author Note:

Medical Disclaimer

This book is not intended as a substitute for the medical advice of your midwife, obstetrician, physician, pediatrician, or other care provider, but rather is meant to supplement, not replace your primary health care person (s). The reader should regularly consult with one of the above care providers in matters relating to his/her health or your baby's health, particularly with respect to any symptoms that may require diagnosis or medical attention. This book has incorporated "Best Practice" guidelines as much as possible and encourages all parents to continue to research the subjects discussed here as new studies are continually being done both here in the U.S. and abroad.

Clarification here

Since I often refer to a mother as 'she' or 'her,' I call most babies in my stories 'he' or 'him,' though I love baby girls just as much and will take any you don't want. Really.

AUTHOR NOTE:

If you find mistakes...

In this or any of my books, please consider that they are there for a purpose. I try to write something for everyone, and some people are always looking for mistakes.

"Thou hast ravished my heart my sister, my bride. Thou hast ravished my heart and given me courage with a single glance...."

Song of Solomon 4:9

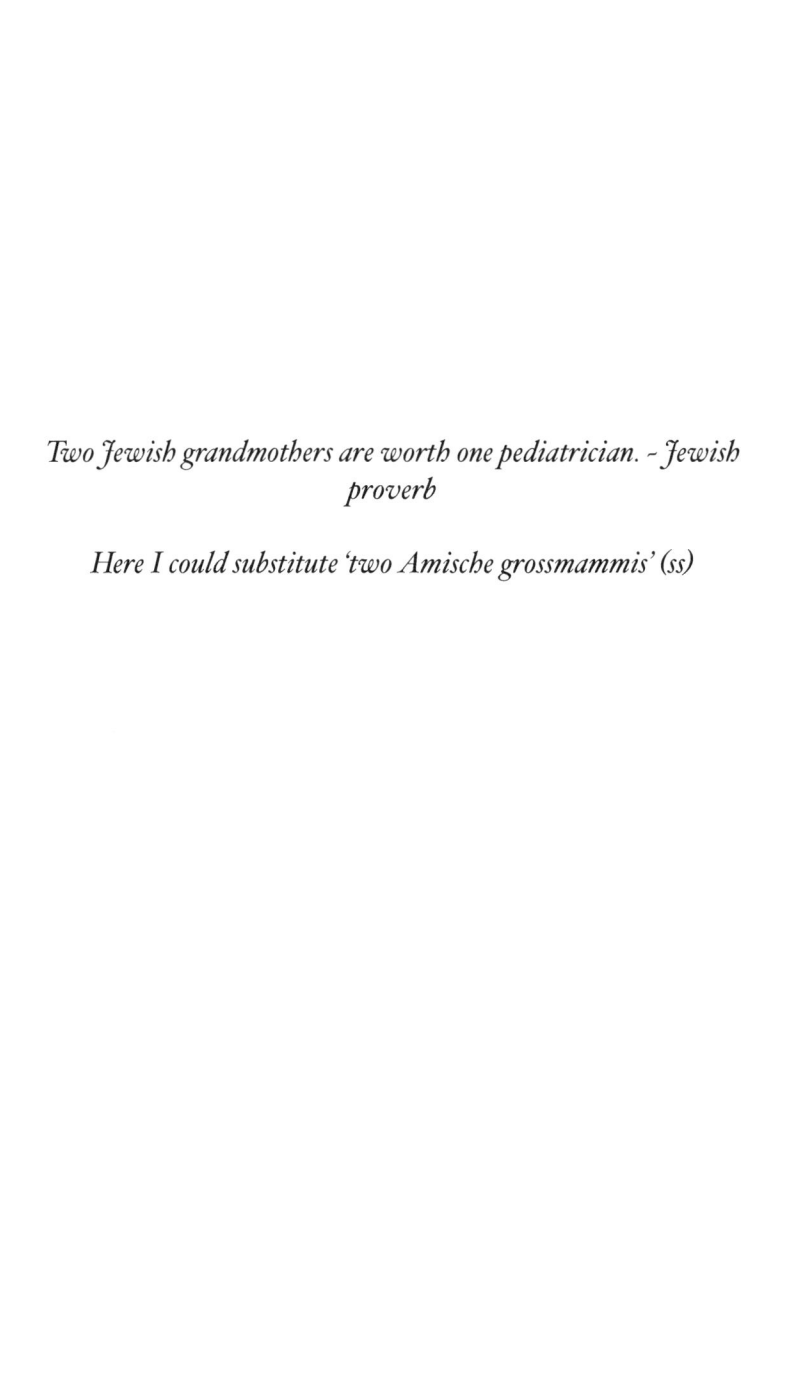

Two Jewish grandmothers are worth one pediatrician. ~ Jewish proverb

Here I could substitute 'two Amische grossmammis' (ss)

The Glossary*

Ach! – Plain expression meaning "Oh!"

Amische – Pennsylvania Dutch dialect word meaning "The Amish."

Bann(s) – Pennsylvania Dutch dialect word meaning "1. public announcement of an upcoming wedding." Also meaning "2. shunning as a path to reconciling with the church."

Baetscher – Pennsylvania Dutch dialect word meaning "bachelor."

Baremlich – Pennsylvania Dutch dialect word meaning "terrible/horrible."

Beheef dich – Pennsylvania Dutch dialect word meaning "behave!"

Bief – Pennsylvania Dutch dialect word meaning "pie."

Bobbel – Pennsylvania Dutch dialect word meaning "baby" singular.

Bobbeli – Pennsylvania Dutch dialect word meaning "babies" plural.

Brot – Pennsylvania Dutch dialect word meaning "proud."

Bruder – Pennsylvania Dutch dialect word meaning "brother."

Buwe – Pennsylvania Dutch dialect word meaning "boys."

Chust – Pennsylvania Dutch dialect word meaning "just."

Dat – Pennsylvania Dutch dialect word referring to or addressing one's "Father."

Daumling – Pennsylvania Dutch dialect word meaning "darling."

Dawdi haus – Pennsylvania Dutch dialect word meaning "a grandparents' apartment usually attached to a main house."

Die gut shtup – Pennsylvania Dutch dialect word for "living room."

Denki – Pennsylvania Dutch dialect word meaning "thank you."

Ditchly – Pennsylvania Dutch dialect word meaning "bandana or work scarf."

Doddy – Pennsylvania Dutch dialect word meaning or when addressing one's "Grandfather."

Eck – Pennsylvania Dutch dialect word meaning "the corner table at a wedding reserved for the couple."

Effe – Pennsylvania Dutch dialect word meaning "off."

Englische (ers) – Pennsylvania Dutch dialect general term meaning "non-Amish."

Esschtick – Pennsylvania Dutch dialect word meaning "lunch."

Ferhoodled – Pennsylvania Dutch dialect word meaning "mixed up or new-fangled."

Frau(s) – Pennsylvania Dutch dialect word meaning "wife/wives, (plural)."

Friede – Pennsylvania Dutch dialect word meaning "friends."

Frolic(s) – Pennsylvania Dutch term for a "scheduled gathering with a single purpose in mind."

Geblumpt – Pennsylvania Dutch dialect word meaning "plump."

Geendt – Pennsylvania Dutch dialect word meaning "eat."

Gemeeschaft – Pennsylvania Dutch dialect word meaning "the congregation."

Glieder – Pennsylvania Dutch dialect word meaning "kitten."

Gott – Pennsylvania Dutch dialect word meaning "God."

Grischtdaag – Pennsylvania Dutch word meaning "Christmas."

Grossmammi – Pennsylvania Dutch dialect word meaning or addressing one's "Grandmother."

Gut – Pennsylvania Dutch dialect word meaning "good."

Halsband – Pennsylvania Dutch dialect word meaning "husband."

Handhawwe – Pennsylvania Dutch dialect word meaning "handsome."

Hannes – Pennsylvania Dutch dialect word meaning "Hands."

Huddlich – Pennsylvania Dutch dialect word meaning "a mess."

Insch – Pennsylvania Dutch dialect word meaning "insane."

Kaffi – Pennsylvania Dutch dialect word meaning "coffee."

Kapp – Pennsylvania Dutch dialect word meaning "prayer cap/bonnet."

Kesselhaus – Pennsylvania Dutch dialect word meaning "wash house."

Kinner – Pennsylvania Dutch dialect word meaning "children."

Ks! – Pennsylvania Dutch dialect word meaning "Go!"

Kumm – Pennsylvania Dutch dialect word meaning "come."

Liebling – Pennsylvania Dutch dialect word meaning "darling."

Liebesbreifs – Pennsylvania Dutch dialect word meaning "love letters."

Mamm – Pennsylvania Dutch dialect word meaning "mother," or "Mom."

Mammi – Pennsylvania Dutch dialect word meaning "Grandma" (familiar.)

Maud – Pennsylvania Dutch dialect word meaning "maid" usually hired.

Meedel – Pennsylvania Dutch dialect word meaning "little girl(s)."

Millich – Pennsylvania Dutch dialect word meaning "milk."

Mosch – Pennsylvania Dutch word meaning "mush" as in hot cornmeal cereal.

Nachen – Pennsylvania Dutch dialect word meaning "a snack."

Onkel – Pennsylvania Dutch dialect word meaning "uncle."

Ordnung – Plain word used by both Hutterites, Amish and Mennonites meaning "the written and unwritten rules and traditions of Plain communities."

Patties down – Pennsylvania Dutch expression meaning "hands folded under the table on laps in preparation for grace."

Redded – Pennsylvania Dutch dialect word meaning "ready/readied."

Roasht – Pennsylvania Dutch dialect word meaning "stuffing with chicken chunks in it, versa a whole roasted chicken or turkey."

Rumspringa – Pennsylvania Dutch dialect word meaning "running around time allowed Amish youth before joining church."

Schnibbles – Pennsylvania Dutch dialect word meaning "little scraps."

Schwesters – Pennsylvania Dutch dialect word meaning "sister(s)."

Shors – Pennsylvania Dutch dialect word meaning "shoes."

Shmuzzling – Pennsylvania Dutch dialect word meaning "hugging and kissing."

Tract – Pennsylvania Dutch dialect word meaning 'traditional dress.'

Vorrot – Pennsylvania Dutch dialect word meaning "food."

Wunderbar-gut – Pennsylvania Dutch dialect word meaning "wonderful and good."

Ya – Pennsylvania Dutch dialect word meaning "yes" or "you."

Yesus – Pennsylvania Dutch dialect word for "Jesus."

Youngie – Pennsylvania Dutch dialect word meaning "the youth."

Yunge – Pennsylvania Dutch dialect word meaning "junk, rubbish."

Zellerich – Pennsylvania Dutch dialect word meaning "celery."

Ztzvilling – Pennsylvania Dutch dialect word meaning "twins."

* Although I have tried to represent Pennsylvania Dutch and local dialects throughout my books as accurately as I can, I am sure my readers who are native speakers will always be able to find fault for which I sincerely ask forgiveness. I know I will never get it perfectly, but I hope you will allow for this. Thank you!

~ Stephanie

Part One

Worrying is like a rocking chair. It gives you something to do but you never get anywhere.
- Erma Bombeck

Tomorrow's world will be shaped by what we teach our children today.
- Amish Proverb

CHAPTER 1
From Afar

His visit was just plain too short. After writing back and forth for an entire year, getting to know each other 'from afar' as they say, Henry had finally visited. It was her fault she wasn't ready to meet him earlier than that. She had decided years ago—eight already—that she wouldn't dare marry again. Only to bury your husband after a buggy accident? There were just too many of those these days. She also decided she wouldn't have more children, after her dear little one died, coming entirely too early and with so many problems. No, she would turn her heart to stone so that nothing could touch it again. Not like that. She'd convinced herself she'd crack up, be a total basket case, no good to anyone, if she had to go through any of that again. No way.

But then the minister took it upon himself to find her a husband. She was still young, only thirty-five. She could marry again. Have children. The minister had received a letter from one of the Amish bishops up in Canada asking about her on behalf of a widower in his district. One thing led to another and unfolded over the past year first into a wonderful friendship and finally brought them to the visit.

Henry hadn't planned it, not at all, but at the last minute had to bring little Rose along, who was all of three years old. Veronica found the precious child irresistible. Rose was always accompanied by her faceless Amish doll she'd named Rosemary, who had little dresses and pinafores matching Rose's. Her mother was in heaven now, though little Rose appeared too young to have understood all the goings on in these last few years, since her birth over three years ago.

Veronica's feelings for Henry had grown during this visit. It became clear that they were indeed meant for each other. *How could* Gott *arrange such things*, she marveled. *Of all the billions of souls in the universe, how could you find that one meant only for you?* She knew it was futile trying to understand any of His ways. They were far too deep and wide for mere mortals to grasp.

She recalled the last day of their visit. Henry was staying with a cousin several miles away from Veronica's farm. Each morning, he and Rose (never without her Amish doll, Rosemary, clutched tightly in her arms) rode over in the cousin's buggy and stayed for most of the day. That last afternoon before he would return to Canada was the hardest. Bittersweet. She had burned the image of him pushing Rose on the swing in the yard into her mind.

Her first husband, Amos, had fixed it up just before their baby was born. She didn't live long enough to use the swing--not once--and Veronica hadn't the heart to take it down in all this time since her dear little Marta's death. And here was Rose laughing her heart out, that deep rolling baby laugh. *I could eat her up; I am hopelessly in love with this little one,* she remembered telling herself that afternoon. Then it struck her. *It should have been my baby swinging there. But maybe,* chust *maybe* Gott *has sent Rose to take her place. To somehow heal the past. Does He really wipe every tear away? It for sure would seem so.*

It had only been a month earlier that she'd gotten the results of the genetic studies from the hospital that confirmed she indeed did *not* carry any genes that could cause future children to be disabled. Her chances of having normal babies were the same as for most other women. She'd only assumed she would lose any future offspring because of what happened the first time. Their baby was premature and the research and technology at the time didn't offer much hope that they could save her. But now, with fear and trembling, she'd written to Henry saying she might be ready for a visit, knowing what she'd found out. Before that he had all but given up hope of moving forward with Veronica and was about to ask the minister's advice to find some new leads in his search for a wife.

They'd shaken hands goodbye on his last day. Neither wanted to be the first to let go. They each knew the unwritten rules of the church concerning dating and honored them, saving more intimate signs of affection for after the wedding. This ensured that one's emotions were kept at bay, that a physical relationship at this stage would only muddle their thinking and take away from each sincerely seeking God's will in this union, together, should it be given.

That last day of the visit was ten days ago now, though it seemed like it had been only yesterday. Veronica felt as if her feet had not yet touched back down to earth; she was still floating on cloud nine. They'd agreed to write until they could come up with a plan for their future together.

Ruth, the Amish midwife in their district had not called

or paged her again since the last birth. Ruth had enlisted Veronica to help her by being a second pair of hands should she have to attend a birth in the district and need an assistant, though Veronica couldn't understand for the life of her why Ruth would ask her. With no experience in such things, she thought of herself as more of a burden, a liability, than a help.

Picking up her coffee mug from the dry sink, she ran her other hand over the length of the still-pristine granite countertop there. Amos brought it on her birthday, the last one before she'd married him, getting her to come out to the buggy and help him haul it in. He explained that it was for her peanut brittle and candy-making business, pointing out that the best chocolates and brittles are cooled on a granite or marble slab. It proved to be true, too. In the end it also proved to be a lasting memory of her dear husband, taken too soon. Far too soon.

She continued to slowly wander through the downstairs rooms of the house. Her parents bought it before she was born, before Rufus, who came along before her. Over the years the snug house had seen several additions added on as the family grew. An annex of sorts off the kitchen, expanding the space there to accommodate them all, where the big oak table fit in was the first renovation. Then a summer kitchen where *Mamm* could cook and do all the canning was erected. It would definitely be an improvement keeping the house cooler during the hottest months. The summer kitchen was basically a pavilion of sorts, with a roof over the cement slab and the walls open to the breeze.

Next came a proper *kesslehaus* where they could concentrate all the washing in one central place for both bodies and clothes. A woodburning stove would keep the room toasty warm and the large kettles of hot water ready. Clothes lines crossed between the rafters there to hang up items during the coldest months, though 'freeze drying' was still *Mamm's* preferred method of choice. She'd hang the trousers and dresses and sheets and larger items outside where the excess rinse water would drip and then freeze the wash quite solid. Freeze dried clothes. The wind did its part too. Pants and all the rest could stand up by themselves then and would be brought in and finish drying inside on the lines.

Next on the tour while sipping her still-warm coffee was *die gut shtup*, the great room or living room. She stopped and gazed at the couch there while wrapping her black wool shawl tighter around herself. *Winter will be here before long*, she mused. *Time to start making* Grischtdaag *presents*. Rosie had fallen asleep there on the last night of their visit. They'd covered her up and returned to the kitchen where they stayed up entirely too late visiting and talking and drinking decaf coffee with a second serving of her rhubarb strawberry pie. Around midnight Henry wrapped Rose up in the blanket and brought her out to the buggy for the trip back to his cousin's house where they'd been staying until they would catch the Greyhound bus back to Canada the next morning.

"I guess this is it," Veronica announced when Henry was finally in the driver's seat.

"I guess it is," Henry replied, "though I hate to leave now. What was it? Three short days?" he asked, shaking his head.

"You'll hurry back once you have everything in order with your *bruder* back in Canada?" Veronica asked.

"Definitely. Then we'll visit your minister together and go from there, *eh?*" Henry said.

"*Ya*. And I will be praying the whole time until I see

both of you again," Veronica assured him, though she was fighting back the stinging tears that were threatening to burst at any moment....

"Me too," he promised in return as he extended his hand. No more words were needed. They both felt it: love. This wasn't some fad or infatuation. Indeed, it was an enduring blessing from a loving Father above.

Learn from the mistakes of others; you can't possibly live long enough to make them all by yourself.
- Amish saying

CHAPTER 2

My Cup Runneth Over

Dear Henry,

Greetings in our dear Lord's Name!

There is so much to say, and then there's nothing to say. It leaves one stunned actually. How does Gott do it? Find chust the perfect mate for each one of us? Such a mystery. My cup runneth over. Psalms 23:5 got that one right, for sure. Never in my wildest dreams could I have imagined...you! I thought I would be content, after all that happened--losing my little baby, and as if that wasn't enough, then losing Amos in a buggy accident—chust living a quiet life here, avoiding any more pain, trying to be grateful each day for the small things I could still do. Silly things really, but little things hopefully done with great love. Like canning for my Amische neighbors. Helping here and there. Even assisting the midwife when she asks for an extra pair of hands. I haven't gotten a call in a while. I still don't know why she even needs me. She is so gut at what she does.

And then you come along into my life. Totally unexpected. Definitely undeserved. Rocking the whole boat, you did. At first, I figured maybe Gott had something in mind here. Only since you've left has it occurred to me that what I thought I wanted or needed only had to do with me. My little orbit. I'd controlled my heart up to that point, all those years, deciding what to let in and what to close myself off to. So utterly controlling. What was safe and what wasn't, ya know? Not exactly about faith, eh? Only this morning did this quote come back to me. I can't even remember where I got it from. I think it is a Swedish saying. "Shared joy is double joy. Shared sorrow is half sorrow."

So, I have been puzzled about this ever since. I think I must be slow—mentally—to figure these things out. It dawned on me that love isn't about only one person. All of a sudden you are sharing. And you aren't carrying your burdens alone. An entirely new dynamic. It's like a whole new life. Where have I been, anyway? I think you cope after a while and try to control your life in such a way as to keep out all the hurt. Or any new hurt. You build walls and they only get higher.

We'll have to talk about going forward now. We didn't even get to practicalities; the visit was so short. I don't have a lot of ideas yet. I am hoping you might.

Please squeeze little Rosie for me. I can't wait to see her again. I adore her. You have no idea. Don't tell her, but I am making a little surprise for her. I plan to mail it when it is finished.

Sending my love and prayers,
Veronica

By the next day Veronica was back to her old routine. Throwing on her robe first thing that morning, she'd run down to the kitchen barefoot and stoked up the wood stove, adding tinder and then a small log on top of the still-warm coals in the firebox. It would soon roar to a good strong fire which would slowly warm the kitchen. Placing the coffee percolator that she had filled the night before directly over the fire, it would soon be bubbling away. Running back upstairs to dress, she made her bed and brushed out her hairs. The same clean ironed outfit still hung on a peg behind the door, should she get a page that Midwife Ruth wanted her to come along to a birth with her and that a hired van was on the way to pick her up.

Time to start making Grischtdaag *gifts,* she told herself as she assembled breakfast fixings back in the kitchen. *I usually start in the Spring. I'm late this year.* Then the thought occurred to her: *If I had a house full of* kinner *I wouldn't be cranking out handmade* Grischtdaag *gifts for everyone year after year, for sure. Will that possibility ever be part of my life? Dear Lord, what do you really have in mind for me? Dare I hope? Only to be disappointed? Why can't I stop hoping? Or being fearful? But then there is Rose. Almost like you're giving my baby back to me by sending her. I love her to the moon and back already. I would be heartbroken if she...if I didn't marry her* dat.

She continued to ponder the possible scenarios before her. Would it even be right to marry Henry just to have Rose as her own? "That wouldn't even be ethical," she admonished herself aloud as she slathered a thick piece of Hobo bread with sweet Amish peanut butter spread. A banana and a mug of coffee with camel milk would complete her breakfast. Only a few months back she'd discovered camel milk. An Amish man in Missouri runs a camel dairy and ships the milk all over the country. It turns out it is the best thing outside of almond or oat or goat milk for those with lactose intolerance. Some don't care for the taste of goat milk and find this more palatable and higher in fat, more like mother's milk for babies. Camel milk is truly one of the finest sources of protein, probiotics, and 'good fats.'

Sitting down at the table she continued thinking about Christmas. Veronica prided herself on knowing she had not bought Christmas presents for over a decade now. Not a one. She wanted to give only truly meaningful gifts for this most holy occasion. Made from a heart of love. Her mind thought back to all the things she'd made in all those years. Useful things that would last, besides. *But,* she thought, *and there is always that but,* eh? *I could have had a house full of* kinner *my now. Eight years later, let me see, there could have been as many as five or maybe six by now if I'd had twins like* Mamm.

Blowing out a long breath she took herself in hand and returned to her original thought: *Grischtdaag* gifts. Last year she'd made twenty-eight pairs of hand-knitted socks. The year before that was The-Year-Of-The-Mittens. She'd collected dozens of wool sweaters from thrift shops and garage and mud sales. Boiling them caused the wool to shrink, tightening the knitting into felt. Then the pattern was cut out of the felt and sewn into mittens. The linings were made from polyester fleece material, also from the thrift stores and garage or mud sales, using the same pattern. Everyone on the list got them along with a tin of peanut brittle.

The wood stove made the best peanut brittle ever. It just didn't get hot enough on the gas stove. No, it had to be made on a wood stove. First you got a rip-roaring fire going in the fire box. It took only minutes to get to a hard crack temperature and be ready to pour onto a greased granite countertop or buttered cookie sheets to cool, scraping the bottom of the pot with a rubber spatula to get the last spoonful there. She didn't even use a thermometer to make it anymore, after that first year. She could tell when it came to exactly the right temperature when the goo sent up a puff of smoke and the edges had a faintly darker tan color. If it had not reached the exact moment that it turned to hard crack, then it would remain slightly gooey and stick in your teeth. No, perfect peanut brittle *has* to be crisp when eaten and crack without being sticky. And it had to be made with shelled Spanish peanuts, the ones with the red papery skins still on the nuts. Each year she still checked if she could see St. Nicholas inside each peanut when she carefully pulled apart the two halves. Her mother had shown her how when she was little, and she still marveled at the little man in there every year. His face was nestled toward the top of the nut. You could always see him there, beard and all.

Veronica had tried to teach Amos how to make peanut brittle the year before they were married. There were only so many places you could go or things you could do together during the coldest parts of the winter when you were dating. Her siblings would join them in the big kitchen, knowing they'd get to be the guinea pigs to test the first batches, (while checking out the new boyfriend.) They were very keen guinea pigs indeed, to say the least. Those first batches would be graded on color, sticky-ness, flavor, thickness and so on. If the guinea pigs were happy, that batch would be rated a success. If it didn't pass, the reject batches went into the cookie jar for the family to consume, which wasn't terrible either.

Amos had come to the house one evening just before supper. *Mamm* had a nice supper planned. She hoped things would work out for Veronica and Amos. She really liked him. So did *Dat*. Amos was kind, dependable, a what-you-see-is-what-you-get kind of fellow. Genuine. He just happened to be quite handsome too, though a girl should definitely not include that as a prerequisite to finding a husband. That would be vanity.

He was always the optimist. Always thinking of others.

This particular evening happened to be Veronica's birthday. Her married sister along with her two sisters-in-law had secretly made a giant cake and ice cream—the ice cream cranked by hand--and planned to descend with their families on the house in time for dessert later that evening.

Amos came to the kitchen door when he had settled his horse in the barn and knocked. Most visitors didn't knock when the lamps were lit, and people were obviously at home. Veronica went to the door and opened it.

"You silly. You don't have to knock, ya know," she began as she held the door and waited for him to go through.

"I know, but I need you to help me with something I got in the buggy. Get your coat on," he directed.

"Whatever?" Veronica asked laughing.

"You'll need your mittens too," he added.

"What is it?" she demanded.

"You'll see," was all he'd commit to.

When they got to the buggy Amos went around to the back and opened the dropdown flap there. A large box lay on the floor with a tiny ribbon in one corner. The box was heavy, he explained, so he needed her to help with it. Sliding it to the very edge of the buggy bed he had her take one side while he hoisted up the other end. They wrestled with the box until they got it as far as the mud room at the kitchen door. Setting it down there, Veronica was nowhere nearer to knowing what he was up to at this point.

"Have you got rocks in here or what?" she whispered.

"Uh-huh," he agreed.

"*Kumm* on. What in the world?" she hissed back. "Can we open it now?" she asked. "I am assuming it is for my birthday?"

"Yup. But not till after supper," he teased.

"What is it, in heaven's name?" she demanded again. "It weighs an absolute ton!"

Amos just smiled. A man of few words he proceeded to pull off his boots after setting the box down in the mud room when they reached the house and washed up at the sink inside the kitchen, greeting *Mamm* then.

Dat was already at the table reading *The Budget*. He looked up and nodded his greeting to Amos. "Hey. What have you got there?" *Dat* queried.

"A surprise," was all Amos would offer.

Dat shrugged and went back to *The Budget*. A minute later he spoke again.

"Here's a *gut* one," *Dat* said as he shook out the paper, chuckling to himself.

"It's from some Yoder in Canada," he began. "The two *buwe* came running in screaming for their *mamm* to *kumm*. 'You gotta *kumm* NOW! Ephram fell into the lake while we were collecting tadpoles. We tried to give him mouth to mouth resuscitation, but he kept jumping up and running away....'" There were several laughs over that one.

"Here's another one," *Dat* continued chuckling. "From New York. 'Several lower-grade boys were having a discussion about Enos Youtzy's new baby boy. They were on the way home from school with a lady driver, sharing the news with her. Said the one, 'The baby's name is Tennis.' 'Oh no,' said the other one. 'His name is Dentist....' (*Dat* paused here, then continued.) '"The baby's name is Dennis Eugene."' Several groans could be heard in the kitchen.

"Here's winner!" *Dat* continued right on.

"Honey, maybe after supper. It's all ready, dear," his wife urged impatiently.

"Okay, okay. *Chust* this one. It's short. From Fredericksburg, Ohio." He read, "'I can hardly believe it's maple syrup time again. A driver and her small son were travelling along a country road. The little son needed the bathroom so bad, and there was none to be had so she did exactly what I would have. She dropped him off close to the woods. When he came back, he said, '*Mamm,* it was so cool, there were even bags hanging on the trees to use,'" Then *Dat* laughed aloud.

Veronica and *Mamm* gasped at the same time when the meaning of the story sunk in. *Mamm* dropped the spoon she was stirring with at the stove just then. It fell with a loud clank.

"*Dat!*" Veronica was mortified. And Amos was right there. What would he think of her family laughing at such a vulgar joke? Everyone else thought it was hysterically funny, Amos included it seemed.

In your prayer it is better for you to have a heart without words than to have words without a heart.
- Amish proverb

CHAPTER 3

The Way of the World

Dearest Veronica,
Greetings in our dear Lord's name!
Your letter brought much joy. I too feel like I've run out of words to describe how I am feeling. I am dumbstruck, basically. How can Gott arrange such amazing things? Well, chust look at the earth, the seasons, the food that feeds us all from such tiny seeds, kinner being born. All miracles. It makes me dizzy thinking about it all.

Rose was chattering to her doll the whole trip back. She asked me several times, "Waernt iss Mamm?" She'd never done that before. Growing up with my bruder's kinner she called Edith, my sister-in-law, mamm along with all the other children. She never knew her mamm. Becky died from complications at the birth. I can't help but wonder if Rose is missing you now. I sure miss you already. I would love to know what goes on in their little heads, wouldn't you?

I remember getting to know her mamm, Becky. Looking back, we were so very young. We were oblivious to any hardships in the future. Everything looked so carefree then. Maybe if we knew what would happen in the future, no one would get married, you know? We'd all become extinct, I'm thinking. I do want to share one thought with you, though. I don't know if you'll agree, but we shouldn't try to forget those we've lost. We shouldn't pretend we don't miss them or mention their names ever again. That wouldn't be gut. They will live in our hearts always, watching us, I believe, from the other side, and even rejoicing in our happiness. I don't believe time heals. Not at all. That's a stupid platitude. It isn't even worth the cost of the embroidery thread to sew it onto a pillow. No, you bring them along with you as go through life. No, secrets and such shouldn't be between us. Not ever. We should be able to share everything.

I am also thinking about what we didn't have time during the short visit to discuss, all sorts of things. I am wondering if you have thought about where we should live? I would like to have you come here to Canada. While I was in the U.S. I wondered about all the liberal ideas I saw there, my cousin's family included. Many in the Amische churches are giving up so many things that have always represented our way of life. Things to make their lives easier, but perhaps letting in too much of the world. I am sure you understand what I mean.

I am thinking that our elders had it right, but each generation seems to find subtle ways to let the world in. I do think that the struggle to stay faithful to the wisdom and foresight of the elders of past generations is playing out now more than ever. I also think we should sit up and take notice. I believe they got this one right. Just look at us now: cell phones, computers at workplaces, so that our lives are now bombarded with a glut of information at every turn. I believe it desensitizes us to where we now think this is all normal. It chips away at our beliefs, before we even know what is happening.

We are closer now, in this generation, than we have ever been, as a church I mean, living more like the English than ever before. Add the cars we hire to take us places. And the time-saving things that are popping up in Amische homes everywhere. Buying frozen foods at the groceries instead of growing and canning our own peas, for example. Gas-powered tractors for one...that shocked me to see on the trip. So what, that some take the rubber off the wheels and think that makes them okay, metal wheels so they can't go out on the highways. The big excuse is that we are competing against Big Ag—large-scale agriculture—so it should be alright. And LED lights everywhere. In our homes, in our buggies, in the workshops. Even wired-up sewing machines now. We mingle with the rest of the world at every chance we can get. Farmers' markets and county fairs. We open our homes to tour buses, for heaven's sake, and offer Amish dinners to scores of tourists, as if they don't know how to make a pie, or chicken and mashed potatoes. What does all this say to our kinner?

I don't think we stop to think about it, what it might do to our children. We should worry about all of it. Even if we say we don't, we do. And it affects every aspect of our lives. Our health, our state of mind, our relationships, our use of time, choice of employment, how we view others and how we prepare our children for living with it, too. These things are not making us better Amische. They are slowly making us more closely aligned with the Englische.

We have always prided ourselves that our way of life will continue while the rest of the world crumbles; the elders often called it 'The Ark,' the church that we have found refuge in, but I think knowing about all the things going on out there is affecting us. Five years ago, I wouldn't have been able to tell you what these words even meant: globalization, climate change, technology, artificial intelligence. All are making huge advances as we speak. Only recently I found out that North Korea is threatening nuclear war, Gaza is being razed to the ground and whole generations in Ukraine and Russia are oblit-

erating each other. I feel so completely helpless to change any of it! Our parents certainly never worried about it.

And that is not all. The Arctic is quickly falling into the sea while fewer green places are surviving, all the while animal life is becoming endangered or extinct. When will it end? Well, the answer is, it won't. It will continue its freefall toward unsustainability if not in our lifetime, then surely during the lifetime of our kinner. Does that make any of it okay since I won't be around to see it and suffer the unimaginable horrors?

I long to become detached from all of this but I can see no way out, though. And I see a real danger in what I saw in the U.S. settlements. Secular newspapers in every home, practically. I am certainly not naïve enough to think we Amische don't have hardships, illness, or stress. But I do think that the struggle to stay faithful to the wisdom and foresight of the elders of past generations is playing out now more than ever.

So then, what next? What choices can each one make? Do we dig in our heels and go on a crusade to save our life and values and separate ourselves even more from those that are embracing modernity? They have plenty of arguments that a little electricity won't hurt their faith, that making their work chust a little easier won't hurt anyone, and that we still live basically apart from the world. I am chust asking if that is enough. I don't believe it is.

The Pandemic is another example. Boy, you should have heard the rows then! For and against vaccines. Pros and cons for shutting down meetings, even Sunday gatherings outdoors no less. What happened to the Bible? Gott telling us that not even one little sparrow will fall without His knowing? But no. Half the church goes running to doctors and follows their advice to get the shots. They are still getting all the boosters, to this day. What does that do to our bodies? To our children? To those not even born yet? And then some saying herd immunity will protect us. What is that, even? Like we are horses and cows or goats. Then the rest who try to believe that Gott sends sickness and death to warn us, teaching us to trust Him alone. Some died here, yes. Maybe it was their time. Who are we to try to control it all? Aren't we trying to play Gott?

And no one seems to be putting a stop to all the nonsense that rumspringa has become. Only a few years ago our parents thought we were wild when we stashed our suspenders in the mailbox or under a bush before going to a barn party or something, retrieving them again before sneaking back into the house later that night. Now the youngie are being tempted with drugs of all sorts and who knows what else? Sex before marriage? Binge drinking?

Sorry I got off on a tangent there. Life was so much simpler only a decade or two ago. What is happening? Who do we believe? Do we go back to the old ways? No chain saws, no hay balers, no running water in the house. Certainly, nix the automatic milking machines. No indoor bathrooms with hot water and gas stoves and refrigerators and kerosene-powered freezers?

So that makes me wonder where we should settle once we're married. I can't help but think we should err on the side of caution. Keep the old ways like here in Canada. What are your thoughts? I trust we will find the way.

With love and prayers,
Henry

Listen, or else your tongue will keep you deaf.
- Amish proverb

CHAPTER 4
Crackers

"Oh, my giddy granny!" Veronica voiced aloud after reading the letter. "I didn't see that one *kumming.*" She carefully folded it up, slid the letter back in its envelope and gingerly laid it back on the table, quickly dropping it there as if it were burning her fingers. "Dang," she swore to herself, and then, *Lord, you gotta step in here...*ferhoodled. *That's what this is. Totally crazy.* Insch *even.*

As if still in shock she slowly slid into her shawl and travelling bonnet, pulled on her sneakers and then took the letter, stuffing it into the purse, and went out to the barn. "Aunt Wanda will know what to do," she whispered to her horse. Her mother's sister was one little bundle of wisdom. Folks often consulted with the octogenarian on a number of problems. Patting the horse, she turned and climbed up into the buggy. "She'll know...." Veronica promised herself as she directed the horse to back up into the yard.

She'd heard the same arguments being discussed even before she was old enough to go to school. She and Amos had also wrestled with the controversies over the years. Sometimes the bishops and ministers voiced their concerns in their Sunday sermons, sometimes it became the supper talk that night. There were always the two camps or more. The quip goes, "Consult with two Amish and you'll get three opinions." One for progress, the others dead set against it. Every year saw at least one family pack up and leave their district to join with either a more progressive church, or a decidedly conservative one. (The process became coined 'migration.') They could join some of the experimental groups out there too, who mixed with Mennonites, some using buggies and others' cars, or a mix of the two. Some adopted more modern dress, giving up the no pockets rules on shirts and trousers, and hooks-and-eyes-only on jackets, or switching to the newer drip-dry polyester dress fabrics. On the other hand, you could also try out the ultra-orthodox Swartzentruber Amish who prided themselves on their stand against all modernizing, claiming that they are still adhering now for hundreds of years to the old ways.

The Swartzentruber Amish are one of the largest and most conservative subgroups of the Amish. They do not worship or intermarry with more liberal Amish groups. The Swartzentruber Amish formed as the result of a division that occurred in Ohio, in the years around 1913–1917. The bishop who broke away was Sam Yoder. The Swartzentruber name was applied later, named after bishop Samuel Swartzentruber who succeeded him. In 1932 there was a split among the Swartzentrubers that resulted in the formation of the Troyer Amish. In the 1980s several church districts in Minnesota, Tennessee, and Ohio split from the Swartzentruber church districts, the splits occurring because disagreement over shunning or the *Bann*, resulting in three Swartzentruber Amish groups. Riding in cars is prohibited among the Swartzentruber Amish, except in emergencies, whereas average Old Order Amish are allowed to use cars as long as they do not own them. Swartzentrubers are the most restrictive concerning the use of technologies among all Amish affiliations.

Remembering Amos, her first husband who had been so abruptly taken from her, made her think about their short time together. They hadn't been married very long when he died in a buggy and car accident. Some elderly man who shouldn't have even been driving at all ran a red light in his fancy car. And that was only a year after their precious baby was born prematurely and died. She'd sworn that she would never marry again, never have children again. No one should have to live with that. She'd be a complete basket case. No, she wouldn't tempt fate, wouldn't even consider such insanity. She'd learned her lesson. She'd be content to live a simple, quiet life without all that drama. Content. That's all she asked for. Not happy really. Just content. She could do content.

Then she continued, this time addressing her horse. "But then some bishop up in Canada stuck his nose into it and got Henry writing to me, and he visits and now this," she told the horse. "Did I have to fall in love with his *bobbel?* Lord, is this a trick? Some awful plan? Predestined even? Marry him and be all submissive, to this and whatever else he can think up? It's enough to turn me into a heretic, for pity's sake." Thus went the conversation in the buggy with herself and the horse the whole way to her aunt's house.

And it continued as she stabled her horse once she got there. "Why can't we *chust* trust the ministers' directions?" she asked while patting the horse, "leave the arguments to them and follow their wisdom? For the sake of peace? But no. The *bruders* want to have their say. Why, even the slow-moving signs on the back of the buggies are up for discussion. They ask 'are they decorations or a genuine safety measure?' What about bonnet strings while we're at it? Too long, too wide, too fancy? Fabric too see-through? Tied, untied? Does the bonnet cover enough of the *fraus'* ears? So, churches split on the subject. Can it get any pettier than that? That's crackers. Absolutely crackers. As if *Gott* has an opinion on such mundane matters. Don't we have better things to do than quibble over it all? I am sure *Gott* does, have better things to do...." she concluded, shaking her head.

And what will Henry think about the million dollars from the widow whose husband ran that red light and crashed into our buggy? I can't imagine what he'll do with that. Make me give it back? Or go hog wild and buy up land, more than anyone really needs? Only the minister and his wife know about it. It would change everything if he knew how rich we'd be. How can I trust that anyone really loves me and doesn't also love all that money? The minister agreed with me that it should stay completely anonymous, that he and I will cosign any checks for a family's medical bills or pay off a farm before foreclosure. The old man's frau insisted. Dorothy was her name. She said he only died in peace because he made her promise something gut might kumm *if it.*

Veronica knocked lightly on the door of the *dawdi haus* where Aunt Wanda lived. It was built onto the old farmhouse as the grandparents' apartment years ago. Now her daughter and her husband lived in the main house with their big family, and she occupied the little bed-sitter. It was a brilliant arrangement. She could walk only the few steps into the big kitchen through the adjoining door and not even have to go outside in inclement weather. There was no answer, so

Veronica knocked again, this time harder. Still no response, so she walked around the porch and knocked on the main house door. Instantly the big door squeaked open and a very tiny little person in a very wrinkled plain brown dress stood there barefoot, staring up at her. He didn't smile or react at all. He just stood there for a moment. Then, quick as a wink he was gone, leaving the front door wide open.

Veronica stepped in and after leaving her shoes on the mat there, called out, "Anybody home?" A volley of giggles went up then. Veronica looked around and noticed three little pairs of bare feet below the hems of the coats hanging on the coat tree to her left. Playing along, she addressed the coat rack. "I'm wondering if anyone lives here. Sure is quiet...." More giggles and then three little people jumped out at her from behind the coats and shawls hanging on the coat stand. Feigning surprise and covering her mouth with both hands made the children jump up and down, ecstatic that they'd fooled her.

Just then their mother came walking down the hall toward the all the noise. Veronica greeted her and took the toddler she was carrying.

"When did this one grow up? He was a newborn last time I was here," Veronica said.

"Well, you feed 'em and they sort of *chust* sprout up on their own," her cousin answered chuckling. "*Ya* know, corn-fed *kinner*."

Then addressing the little band of troublemakers Veronica asked, "And who is this?"

The biggest one stood up straighter and lisped, "I'm Chassua." His mother stepped in and explained. "That's Joshua, and this one next to him is Pauline," and before she could continue the last one ran and hid behind her mother's skirt. Rhoda turned around slightly and said, "Oh, and that's

Sylvia. She's shy. *Chust* follows the others everywhere. And you know that one," she continued, nodding her chin at the child in Veronica's arms. "That's Clarence. Already almost a year now."

"So that's four, *eh?*" Veronica asked. "That leaves the one that answered the door."

"Yes. Harold. He's almost four," she explained. "He's most likely back in the kitchen behind the cookstove with the bitty goat. We're bottle feeding it. A runt. The *mamm* rejected it. Harold has adopted it, it seems. He barely leaves it alone all day. He smells like it now, too," she added laughing as she scrunched up her nose. "He'll outgrow his baby dress pretty soon and then all his clothes will all smell like goats, too," she moaned.

"Oh, ugh," Veronica groaned and then explained the reason for her visit. "I came by to see Aunt Wanda. Is she home?"

The three little urchins instantly made a mad dash toward the *dawdi haus* door, getting themselves wedged in the doorway before untangling themselves and forging ahead while ignoring their mother's orders not to wake the old lady should they find her sleeping.

"She's probably *chust* reading or resting," Rhoda guessed, shaking her head. "*Kumm* in. Will you have some *kaffi* with me?"

Veronica hung her shawl and black travelling bonnet on a peg in the hallway and followed Rhoda into the expansive kitchen. Settling herself at the table with Clarence on her lap she commented, "I don't know how you do it, Rhoda. Five *kinner*."

Rhoda set down a mug of steaming coffee in front of Veronica while shyly adding, "and another one by *Grischtdaag*. We feel so blessed, actually. Healthy *kinner*, a *gut* farm, church with *bruders* and *schwesters*, a *gut* marriage. *Gott* is good, Veronica."

As she was cutting a large wedge of French rhubarb pie for her guest, Rhoda gazed at Veronica from across the table.

"And what has He done in your life *chust* now? Did you *kumm* this way to tell us some news perhaps?"

Veronica paused to collect her thoughts. So many were swirling 'round and 'round in her head at that moment. Finally, she said with a deep sigh, "Well, I don't know where to begin...."

Two great talkers will not travel very far together.
- Amish saying

CHAPTER 5
Peppa Pig

"Well? What is she like? Did you two hit it off? Does that smile tell me there's a wedding *kumming* soon?" Henry's brother, Milo, followed him into the house, right on his heels, as soon as he heard him come in from the van they'd hired to pick him up at the bus station.

"Well, tell me!" Milo practically shouted while cornering Henry by the coat pegs.

"Hold your horses," Henry grumbled back at him. "Let me get settled here, will y*a?* I haven't even put Rosie down, youse," he shot back. Henry pulled off her shoes and socks and tossed them onto the mat by the back door. Then setting Rose on her feet and smoothing down the hem of her dress, he reached into his huge inside vest pocket and pulled out Rose's doll and handed it to her.

"Denki," she answered politely before dashing off to greet her little cousins.

Edith was cooking in the kitchen as the two brothers came in. Henry's bags and suitcases were dumped as he headed for the table and sat down heavily.

"Whew. That is one long trip," Henry exclaimed while

wiping off his forehead with his bandana handkerchief. "Twenty-six hours with a three-year-old. She was as *gut* as gold, mind you, but we must have read every one of her books at least a dozen times. I am not kidding. I could probably recite *Peppa Pig* by heart now. That dang bus stopped at every town along the entire route. They told us which ones we could get out at and stretch or get a sandwich, but other than that it was non-stop, and we couldn't get off."

Milo's oldest son was eight. He silently slid onto the bench at the table opposite Henry while Edith set a big mug of steaming creamy coffee in front of Henry.

"Supper will be ready pretty soon," she told him. "Are ya hungry?" she inquired.

Henry nodded as he took a long swig from the mug. Lester took the opportunity to ask a question. "Did they have a bathroom on the bus?" he wanted to know.

"Yes, but it was stinky," Henry answered after he'd swallowed. "Tons of perfume spray or something I'm guessing. You can't breathe in there. It makes you homesick for our old outhouse," he chuckled.

"Did you see any interesting folks?" Lester continued.

"Ya, a few." Henry sat back and took another draught from his mug. "A bunch of Hutterites—they're the ones that their *fraus* wear all those polka dotted scarves—who kept to themselves, and some missionary group that sang half the night away till the bus driver told them to shut up and be quiet 'cause people wanted to sleep...oh, and a couple that had a baby that screamed her head off for a couple of hours. They kept pouring Coca Cola into her bottle. Poor thing. You can't tell them anything, though you sure wonder why some people wanna have *kinner* at all...." he pondered aloud. "Yup, you see all sorts. One kid got on the bus and was escorted off at the very next stop where two police officers were waiting for him on the loading dock for smoking marijuana in the biffy on the bus. That driver sure was upset about that. He must've radioed ahead to call the cops. Oh, and two nuns in their getup who were really nice and kept giving Rosie cookies and talking to us. They didn't have a clue Rosie won't talk English until she gets to first grade." They all chuckled at that.

Supper was ready and Edith called the rest of the family to come. They lined up to wash their hands and finally all were settled at the table. After a very abbreviated silent prayer, shorter than usual, Milo again began the barrage of questions for Henry once more.

"Settle down," Henry told him as he reached for the breadbasket in front of him. Taking a slice, he slathered on a generous layer of sweet Amish peanut butter spread and proceeded to cut the slice into little cubes which he sprinkled in Rose's little plastic bowl on her highchair tray while Edith tied a bib on her. Then she returned to the wood stove and brought the last platters to the table.

The table was covered with a floral-patterned oil cloth. A single Coleman lantern hung above it from a chain in the ceiling. There was a bench along the old oak table by the back wall where the seven children were all waiting silently. Their hands were still folded in their laps from the preceding prayer. Their mother began taking plates from a stack at the foot of the table and filling them, passing them along to each one of the children. This was a festive meal, a bit more generous than a regular weekday supper. Henry had come home. And Rose. Edith knew which of the two she had missed the most.

As the bowls and casserole dishes were sent around first to Milo and Henry the platters finally settled somewhere along the middle of the table, below the lantern. Shadows played on the walls as the sun sank along the horizon, casting fewer and fewer rays into the cozy kitchen until the sky went dark.

The counters were tidy, very little *yunge* cluttering any surface there. A set of matching canisters with their accompanying matching labels sat along the back of the counter. One end of the space held a row of jars with lentils, beans, and seeds in various stages of sprouting, their metal mesh lids allowing for a daily rinse. A large aluminum bowl loosely covered with a flour sack towel on the dry sink held a sourdough sponge that was working its magic which would be transformed into yeasty buckwheat waffles in the morning. The older children had worked hard bringing in the maple sap earlier that year, tapping hundreds of trees and boiling it down to just the right consistency for syrup which surprisingly yielded quite a crop. The quart jars filled with the precious amber liquid lined a whole shelf in the root cellar below the kitchen.

Regulation blue curtains hung in the windows on three sides of the large kitchen. An extension had been built onto the house as the number of little helpers increased over the years. A handmade clock hung in the center of one wall there, ticking loudly. In the center of an adjacent wall hung a calendar with a John Deere tractor pictured on it. A collection of vintage blue mason jars of various sizes stood atop the Dutch cupboard in a tidy row. The 'good' dishes were stacked neatly inside the cupboard.

Little treasures had made their way to the cupboard over the years for safekeeping: a handful of stone arrowheads, a Valentine's Day card, and a pair of cutglass goblets commemorating the fiftieth wedding anniversary of their parents. The tall cupboard had been Milo's wedding gift to Edith, which he had built from cherry wood with gingerbread trim and cornices crowning the upper shelves. Someone along the way had fashioned oiled brown shelf paper from grocery bags which hung over the front of each shelf not more than three inches with a simple scalloped-designed edge and eyelet-style hole-punched flowers.

Henry hadn't finished his first mouthful of chicken before Milo lit into him again. "So, what is she like? Tell me!" he demanded. Without waiting for an answer, he forged on.

"Any *kinner*? Is she like, um... needy?... shy? ...attractive?"

Henry glared back at him and continued chewing, refusing to entertain his brother's curiosity. His wife thought she'd defuse the situation and asked gently,

"Well, what did Rosie think of her?"

Henry's look practically sent daggers into the two of them. Taking a long swig from his mug he held it up for seconds. Edith obliged, popping up from the table and grabbing the coffee pot from the back of the stove top.

"I'll get the *millich*," she offered.

Then Milo piped up. "Hey, what is this anyway?" he asked as he raised a casserole dish to his nose and sniffed. "Is it *gut* for me...or will I like it?" he demanded, half joshing. "Can't be both."

"It's from Maudie's column in *The Budget*. It looked real *gut*," Edith informed him. "It's called 'Potato Haystack Baked Casserole.' Let me know if it's a keeper, okay?"

"Well, there have been a few disasters from her, ya know," he stated skeptically.

"No, there haven't now," she protested. "Well, one," she revised her answer. "They didn't like the cold beef tongue spread on toast, did they? The one that you grind up with apples and pickles. I won't try that one again. I promise," she humbly stated. Then as an afterthought she added, "but this week Maudie had an interesting recipe from Indiana for fried dandelion blossoms...." Before she could continue, a unanimous groan rose up from the children lined up on the opposite side of the table on the bench. Their loud 'Nooooooo!' reverberated throughout the kitchen.

"Okay. I can take a hint," she backed down.

The Budget is a weekly newspaper that connects all the Plain communities throughout North and South America founded in Ohio in 1890. Without telephones or radios, it is the next best thing to keep abreast of all the news in the Amish world. A scribe is assigned in each community or district and faithfully writes all the news fit to be printed once a week. Weddings, important gatherings, new babies, deaths—it's all in there. Maudie has been writing her column and including recipes since the early 1980s.

Lester couldn't keep quiet one more second. "Did you see any cowboys *Onkel* Henry?" he asked.

"No," he answered laughing. "Some horses, though. My cousin, where I stayed, had some mighty fine Percherons. Nicest ones I've seen in a long time. A really long time. They're pretty modern down there though. I was surprised actually. Electricity in their bulk food store and dairy room, indoor bathrooms, gas-powered hay baler, and automatic washing machines. Milking machines, too. I was shocked, to tell the truth. I'm not sure that is progress," he said, shaking his head.

"But lots are going that way, saying it doesn't affect how they live and what they believe. I think it is insidious, sneaks in before you know it," Edith added. "First, they *chust* say, 'Oh we're competing against Bid Ag and it'll help us produce more.' And then they *chust* think, 'But if I have electricity then I can check the weather on the radio and not loose so much crop to rain and storms or keep up with world news." Or they say, 'If only I had a blender and a juicer I could make so many healthier things,' and before you know it, you've got air fryers and an electric stove, and an electric food dehydrator, a hair dryer and a toaster—all in the name of progress and health—oh, and the car, *'chust* for emergencies,' they say, and then a computer for the teacher to research more classes and prepare the scholars for the new technology in the world.... When will it ever end? You've spent a whole lot of money buying all this *stuff* that's supposed to save you time and money so you can go on more trips and visits, all well and *gut.*" At that she jumped up from the table, saying, "hang on a minute. I *chust* read this recently, I'll go get it," she said as she left the room.

Returning a minute later, she quickly sat back down and began. "My cousin sent it in her last letter. She found it in their little library. It's from some Buddhist publication, she says. Don't know why for the life of me she's reading that stuff, anyhow," she mused, shaking her head. "But here, I'll read it," she began. "It's called, 'The Paradox of Our Age.'

> "We have bigger houses but smaller families.
> More conveniences, but less time.
> We have more degrees, but less sense, more knowledge but less judgement.
> More experts, but more problems; more medicines, but less healthiness.
> We've been all the way to the moon and back but have trouble crossing the street to meet the new neighbor.
> We built more computers to hold more information to produce more copies than ever but have less communication.
> We have become long on quantity but short on quality.

> These are times of fast foods but slow digestion.
> Tall men but short character.
> Steep profits but shallow relationships.
> It's a time when there is much in the window, but nothing in the room."

The kitchen was silent then, all taking this in.

"He's for sure got that right," Henry said while shaking his head and reaching for the chicken platter to his right. "I don't know anything about those Buddhists, but that is spot-on, eh?"

Again, the silence stretched out into the room. A minute passed. You could hear a pin drop.

Then Rosie's tiny voice could be heard as she slowly, haltingly, sang her favorite song that her *dat* sang to her each night before tucking her in: "...In the na-ame of Jesus, Je-e-sus, we have the vic-tor-y!" Then she was quiet too. Her cheeky little smile had returned. Then dipping her head and holding up her Benjamin Bunny bowl with both hands she asked sweetly, "More, please."

Consider using soft words and hard arguments.
- Amish saying

CHAPTER 6

Flying Squirrels

Aunt Wanda shuffled into the big kitchen just as all the children bolted past her to resume their games. It was sprinkling outside, so they were stuck indoors for now. The little herd headed for the back bedroom to think up their next prank, satisfied with themselves that they'd managed to surprise their guest. They sat on the bed, on the floor and on the one chair there, the girls fondling their faceless dolls, the boys catching their breath before the next escapade.

Aunt Wanda had just turned eighty-two. She was a spry old thing, not looking at all like the wizened old woman you'd expect at that age. She'd raised her ten children in the big house with her doting husband Ray. For the most part they lived a happy, though not-so-peaceful life. There was always some drama; just as you fixed the last episode and thought you'd evade the next hurdle for a little while, at least. Four woodchoppers and six dishwashers they'd had, the Amish designations when announcing the latest arrival from the stork for friends and family. Matters of birth and death were basically out-of-bounds topics when raising *youngie*. In general, questions about such subjects were relegated to the "I'll tell you when you're old enough" ever-growing list of mysterious matters. *Kinner* were always curious, but compliant when their endless questions were redirected over and over again to the nether world of the unexplained hinterlands for now.

Veronica waited until Rhoda had finished her coffee and the dear *grossmammi* had drained her mug and asked Aunt Wanda if she could talk to her in private. Rhoda smiled sweetly and said, "you'll let me know if there's any news, won't ya?" as the other two left the kitchen through the door to the *dawdi haus*.

"Make yourself comfortable," her aunt instructed Veronica as she picked up the newspaper she had been reading and began folding it up until she remembered a story she had just read when the children stormed in. "You gotta let me read this one to you, dear," Aunt Wanda said as she again opened the paper. "Oh, where is it? Did you read *The Budget* today yet?" she asked as she hunted for the story. "Oh, I found it," she said as she sat down in the bent hickory rocking chair by the tiny loveseat where Veronica had settled.

"It's from Iowa," she began reading aloud. "'John Hostellers had one pesky squirrel come to their sunflower feeder quite regularly and go right by the ear corn they had put out for him. Sara had tried several things to keep him from the feeder. The other day it was snowing and very windy, and sure enough he was at that feeder and had his back turned towards the house and tail dangling down over the side of the feeder, munching away on the sunflower seeds. And then Sara came up with a new plan.

"She bundled up for the cold and ever so softly out the door she went with her eyes on that squirrel's tail hanging over the side of the feeder. Unaware of his plight, Sara grabbed that tail and in one quick motion Mr. Squirrel found himself sailing out across the yard and hasn't been back since for sunflower seeds!'" Aunt Wanda chuckled at that and went back to folding up the paper and set it on the little table by her chair. Then brushing her apron out flat, folded her hands in her lap as she gazed at Veronica. Not one to beat around the bush, she asked, "So, to what do I owe this visit?"

"Oh, I don't know where to begin. Well, here. It came this morning," Veronica said as she produced the letter from her purse, her voice cracking, breathing out a long sigh.

Aunt Wanda moved her glasses higher up on her nose and began reading. At the end of page one she looked up at Veronica and stated simply, "Mercy me!" her eyebrows raised as far up as they could go. Veronica nodded. Then Aunt Wanda went back to reading the voluminous rant on the next two pages while Veronica studied the intricate patterns in the faux barn wood plank flooring, all the time wringing the hem of her apron. The grandmother finished and folding it up, tucked the letter neatly back into the envelope. Shaking her head, she continued pondering what she could say. What *should* she say? She sensed there was no hurry to 'fix' this, that divine wisdom was somehow the only thing that could sort it all out, and definitely prayer seeking some divine intervention from above.

"And this is the feller you were getting to know all that time? He visited, too?" Wanda asked. Veronica nodded her answer. Then Aunt Wanda continued. "And this was the first hint of what he believes?"

"Well, we agreed on everything else. The important things. The things I thought were important at least: straight speaking, honesty, staying in the *Amische* church and the *Ordnung,* raising *kinner* our way, hard work, respecting and caring for our old folks, ya know?" Aunt Wanda nodded in agreement. Then Veronica continued.

"But this *kumms* out of the blue. We didn't really decide where we want to settle after we marry. I assumed—perhaps wrongly—that we'd live here, near my family. He only has his *bruder* in Canada and their passel of *kinner*."

"It's the same ol' story, I'm afraid. Everyone thinks they know which way is right, where the grass is greener. I think," Aunt Wanda paused to collect her thoughts then, taking off her glasses and rubbing her eyes with the palms of her hands, as if to erase the words she'd just read, if that were even possible. "I think it doesn't matter at all in the end. The little things, ya know, bonnet strings and buggy signs and where the bathroom is or isn't won't make us holy. Whichever way the church thinks is best is right for them, what they agreed to. But it is the way we live it, day in and day out. You can have hypocrites and drunks in the most observant settlements, and adulterers and liars in the most progressive groups. What matters is what is in each one's heart. *Gott* knows. He sees it. We can't fool Him by looking all pious and churchy and spouting all holier-than-thou religion. You can do it all the old way and get mighty proud of your austerity, or you could try this new thing or that, but maybe you'll be humble enough down the road to realize it is a bit too modern and not necessary and have the humility to rethink that direction. I doubt saints are made by pushing a plow by hand and cussing the whole time, with a flask of hooch hidden in the back pocket of your overalls, but they aren't made by giant combines either. We'll have to ask for guidance on this one, dear," Aunt Wanda concluded, reaching her hand out to cover Veronica's. Then as she popped up from the rocker, she asked, "Tea or *kafffi?* We'll have some *esschtick*. I have a lovely quiche we can have for lunch, leftovers from yesterday. And one of my granddaughters made me a sour cream crumb pie, don't ya know. It was one of Maudie's in *The Budget*. I can't eat it all by myself now, can I?" she stated.

Veronica had been hoping for some wisdom from her aunt. Something that would fix it all. *Dear Lord,* she began thinking to herself. *Please show us the way. Please.*

> *Prayer is the key of the dawn and the bolt of dusk.*
> *- Amish saying*

CHAPTER 7
Multi-tasking

The next day was fully booked before she even got up. Every week Veronica went to one of her elderly *onkel's* and aunt's *dawdi haus* to clean and cook for them. Other relatives signed up for the other days so no one person was tied down all the time, but the old folks were never neglected.

Eli and Hazel never had children to look after them in their old age. The day often included a trip to the doctor and of course ice cream after that—since they were in town anyway. Not having electricity limited the times you could have ice cream with no way to keep it frozen at home unless you had one of those very expensive kerosene freezers. If you were in town, though, it was taken for granted you'd get to indulge in ice cream. Sometimes families stopped on the way home after a shopping trip and bought ice cream and passing out spoons when you got home, you could all eat it out of the gallon pail till it was gone. Any leftovers would turn to soup and be wasted, again unless you had a freezer.

Sometimes they'd hire a driver to take them to the next town where they could also shop at the thrift stores there.

You never knew what little treasures you'd find. Amish romance paperbacks, and cooking and craft books were available for just pennies and were on the top of the list. Once you found a new romance (albeit clean) paperback it would certainly cycle through all the women in the district. The novels were few and far between. Some *fraus* read the same book three and four times before newer ones were circulated. Some of the baby clothes at the thrift stores looked brand new, barely worn at all. For under a dollar, you might find a little onesie suit or baby socks for nieces and nephews. Even Gohn Brothers' catalog from Middlebury, Indiana couldn't beat those prices.

Today Veronica would bring along two loaves of Hobo bread and a pan of sourdough cinnamon rolls she'd made at home yesterday, baking for them being one task she could check off the to-do list this morning for the old folks. She quickly dressed and went to the kitchen to stoke up the wood stove to heat water for coffee. She hurriedly made a peanut butter and jam sandwich. By the time that was done she filled her to-go thermal travel mug with coffee, pouring in some camel milk and screwed on the top. She'd have breakfast on the way to save time. Grabbing the two bags with the bread and the pan of rolls she headed for the barn. She was getting the hang of multi-tasking lately. There were only so many hours in a day to do all the things she'd planned. She reviewed the list as she went to hitch up her buggy.

The last of the garden needed picking and canning. Green tomato relish. Garlic dilly green tomato pickle with the tiniest ones. The last squash, pumpkins and kale could go in the root cellar, though she had at least a couple of weeks before the first hard frost she figured.

The set of matching quilted sofa pillows for her niece's wedding gift needed some attention. They were almost done. The yard needed a cleanup day before it would become a real mess. Bushes need trimming. Leaves needed raking up, burning the whole pile then. The picket fence could use a new coat of whitewash. The porch was screaming for a fresh coat of paint. The two sheep needed sheering before it turned colder so they could at least re-grow a good fleece before the first snow. *Get the neighbor to kumm for them,* she told herself.

Then there were the herbs. Oregano, tarragon, basil, peppermint, lemon balm, lavender, chocolate mint, dill, bay leaves, chives, and sage. This would be the third and last cutting of the herbs. They would be hung up on the home-made rack she'd fashioned behind the wood stove's stovepipe, not close enough to cook, but warm enough to effectively dehydrate before being put into jars.

And then there was a reply to write to Henry. Whatever could she say? What would she say? *I didn't bank on going into battle over this. How do you even address such a tirade? Is this gonna be a deal breaker?* she asked herself. *How sad to throw it all out the window over such nonsense. Is this gonna be me against him? What he thinks is best for the both of us? And I am chust submissive and go along with it all? Even if I disagree? Even if I don't believe in it?*

That last letter literally hit her like a ton of bricks. Did relationships really have to include such heartbreak? Would their friendship survive this newest wrench in the whole thing? At this point she doubted that it would. Survive. And it was all going so well...until now.

Aunt Wanda told me that you should marry your best friend, she mused. *That would ensure a good marriage. But what if your intended suddenly dumped such a mess back on you? I'd had no warning. We agreed we felt so united on the day he left with Rose to travel back to his home in Canada. Where did this even kumm from? I was better off before this all began. Content. Not wanting any more. What have I gotten myself into? Why couldn't I chust be satisfied being single? I was, ya know.*

For goodness sakes, she thought, as she climbed up onto the bench, putting her breakfast things into the plastic cup caddy she'd screwed onto the dashboard, wedged her purse behind her feet and backed the horse out to the drive. The two loaves and the pan of buns were on the seat next to her. *There are wars, famine, children dying across the world and we're arguing about slow-moving signs and reflector tape on buggies, and indoor bathrooms? There's got to be some clear sign pointing us to how* Gott *would have us live. In peace and harmony. Not all this strife and discontent. But how do we find it? This legalistic thinking won't bear gut fruit. We hear in sermons that in these times we must live by the Spirit. Love our neighbor. Be present to that one right in front of you. Help them, love them. That He will guide us, as a church and individually. Prayer and fasting. That's what I'll do. Dear Jesus, only You know how to fix this. I don't have a clue. I am giving this all up to You. Do with me whatever is best. And take care of Henry and Rose. I love them both, but I can't see my way through* chust *now.*

She took a huge bite of the sandwich and drank some coffee to console herself. *And I can't even fast for five minutes* she told herself while taking another monster bite from the sandwich. She swiped her lips with the back of her hand. With a flick of the reins, she was off.

Eli and Hazel were waiting for Veronica, enjoying a second cup of coffee in the tiny kitchen of the *dawdi haus*. They were sharing sections of *The Budget* newspaper, Eli reading about a new Amish settlement in Maine, she scanning a lengthy essay entitled, 'Just Plain Mom.'

The little apartment looked well lived in. There were

two recliners in the back half of the room, both with colorful homemade Afghans thrown over the backs of them. On the floor next to one chair a stack of newspapers was teetering precariously, threatening to erupt at any moment. Slumped by the other chair lay a carpet bag with its contents spilling over the top edge: knitting needles, skeins of wool and the beginnings of what already looked like a child's sweater. An antique bent wood hickory rocker was squeezed next to the door to the main house. A small version of a hutch cupboard filled with a lifetime of dishes —but only the ones that had survived a whole generation without breaking--and little treasures stood nearby. On top of the cupboard was a neat row of blue glass vases, some holding an array of silk and plastic flowers.

The breakfast dishes and apparently also the plates and pots from the last meal from the day before were piled up by the sink to the right of the cast iron water pump. It was piped in directly to the tiny kitchenette. A miniature kerosene stove with only two burners stood on the other side of the room and an ice chest was tucked into the corner nearby. A small round table with two matching chairs sat in the center of the kitchen area. The bed was half hidden in an alcove off of that room. An old double wedding band quilt covered the bed. A mantle kerosene lamp sat on a nightstand.

"Help yourself to *kaffi,* dear," Hazel called to Veronica who was hanging her things in the mud room.

"I'm fine, thank you though," Veronica called back. She came into the kitchen and set the pan of sweet rolls on the table. She found a pie server in the utensil drawer and set that by the pan with a short stack of pie plates from the cupboard.

"Ooooh. Those do look yummy," Hazel agreed shuffling over to the table. At the mention of food Eli slowly raised himself out of his chair and staggered over to the table with the help of his cane, where he plunked himself down also, letting the can drop to the floor with a clatter. Hazel watched as Eli didn't wait for an invitation to sample this treat but lifted out a gooey roll with the pie server, oblivious to the fact that he was drizzling glaze on the tablecloth along the way to his plate.

"But I *chust* had breakfast so I'll save mine for lunch. You still have room Eli? After all that fried corn *mosch?* Mercy me!" Hazel said.

"I baked yesterday so we'll have more time today. So, what's on your schedule?" Veronica wanted to know as she settled herself and sat on a little step stool.

"Oh, well, let's see. I have a short grocery list. We can pick those things up at Nordic Sales up in Plymouth and some cloth from them, too," Hazel said. "I am making some things for the next mud sale. It's fun to see all the people who come, ain't? And we have Dorcas' wedding *kumming* up too. Are you making them something?" Hazel wanted to know.

"I've almost finished sewing a set of quilted pillows for them," Veronica informed her. "Tulip garden. One of my favorites."

"So, any news? We feel so cut off here some days," Hazel began. "The weather hasn't cooperated much either lately, though we get it second hand from all those that visit us, the news that it. Did you know Gretchen—Phillip's Gretchen—fell down the basement stairs yesterday? I am sure that'll make it into *The Budget* next week. She's no spring chicken either. There was this leak in the roof over the mud room where the stairs go down, and they were all wet and she didn't see that because she didn't bring along the flashlight, and down she goes. Got banged up pretty badly but no broken bones, at least, praise the Lord. The grandkids say she looks like a raccoon. Two black eyes. Poor dear!"

"Oh, that's horrible. They've got plenty of grown *kinner* to help out, don't they?" Veronica asked. "Vanessa and Samatha are still home I think."

"That's right. And she won't have to worry about cooking or cleaning for now," Hazel agreed. "That's a blessing in itself."

"And tell me, how are you? The fellow back in Canada now? What's his name?" Hazel wanted to know.

"Henry. Well, I am not sure we'll find our way through this latest muddle. Things were going really well, I thought. He visited, and I love them both dearly. Rose is almost four and an absolute angel. We had a wonderful couple of days before they went back. So then, see, he wrote an impossibly long letter when he got back, arguing about this and that; I did not see that *kumming*. I brought it along if you'd like to see it. Maybe, you'll have some wisdom for me," she said as she took the offending letter out of her purse. "I can't begin to recount everything. It's all in there, though," she said as she handed the envelope to Hazel. Then she went in search of her handkerchief and honked into it after first wiping her eyes.

Trust in God, but keep your camel tied tight.
- Amish saying

CHAPTER 8

Waernt iss Mamm?

There was another letter in the mailbox the very next day.

Dearest Veronica,
 Greetings of Love in our dear Lord's Name!
 Most of the seedlings are set out now. The kitchen garden is full, even weeded. The kinner *are responsible for that. Edith actually keeps a logbook for the garden over the years. She notes how many rows they've planted and what's out there. Then she lists all the seedlings, how many rows we set out. There's all the statistics of how many bushels we harvest and how many quarts of all they've canned. How many jars of tomato sauce, pickles, ketchup, salsa, jam and what have you. Then before she starts the seedlings in the greenhouse in February, she goes down to the root cellar to count how many quart jars of what are still left, what she might have canned surplus of. Like, if there are still twelve jars of chow-chow pickle, she knows she can probably make a few less this year, use up the old ones first and then plant a bit less of all the vegetables that'll go into it. She also has a chart of what she thinks she needs each year, like,*

how many jars of dill pickles she thinks we'll use in a week and then does the math, calculating how many jars she uses in a week on average, multiplying that by fifty-two weeks in a year, reckoning on serving the church lunch here twice a year at the most—counting that extra in, maybe six or seven jars, and projecting the numbers from there. She's a proper accountant.

"*Her chow-chow won a ribbon at the county fair up here last year. I am not surprised. I have never tasted better, ya know? I am including her top-secret recipe here. Please do not share it. I really enjoyed your cooking while I was there. I saw a funny supposedly Amish saying a while back: It says, "Kissin' don't last. Cookin' do" and the other one: "'The way to a man's heart is through his stomach'. Well, at least a gut cook helps....*"

Edith's Famous Chow-chow

6 large green tomatoes or six small green ones
3 large yellow or white onions
3 medium red, yellow, or orange bell peppers or all kinds
1 large green bell pepper
½ medium head cabbage (about 4 cups after chopping)
¼ cup sea salt, pickling salt, or kosher salt, not table salt because it usually contains iodine.
3 ½ cups white vinegar (OK with cider vinegar)
1 cup sugar or honey
1 tablespoon mustard seeds
1 teaspoon dry celery seeds
1 teaspoon each turmeric and ground cloves

It is easy to double or triple this recipe. First stem the tomatoes, coring if needed, and quarter. Peel the onions and cut them all into quarters. Stem and seed the peppers and quarter. Core the cabbage, quarter, and set aside.

Use a hand-crank food mill or grind them in a food

grinder fitted with the coarse die to chop each vegetable into fine pieces.

Once all the vegetables are chopped, sprinkle the salt over the top. Using clean hands, mix everything thoroughly, making sure to mix all the vegetables and reach to the bottom of the bowl.

Cover and keep cool overnight. Then place in a colander, and drain, pressing lightly on the mixture with the back of a spoon. Do not rinse. Set aside.

Prepare the brine in a large non-reactive pot. Add the vinegar, sugar, mustard, dried celery seeds, turmeric and cloves and bring to a boil. Once boiling, lower the heat to a strong simmer, cover, and allow to simmer for 10 minutes.

Cook the relish and can:

Add the chopped vegetables to the vinegar mixture, stir, and bring back to a boil. Once boiling, set a timer for 10 minutes and stir often, adjusting the heat as necessary to make sure nothing sticks to the bottom of the pot.

Remove the relish from the heat and fill each jar with the chow-chow, leaving ½ inch of headspace at the top of each jar (about the depth of the lip and jar screw threads). Carefully wipe each jar lip with a clean, dry cloth or paper towel, then top with a clean lid and screw on the band so it is finger tight. Repeat.

Process the chow-chow: bring your water bath to a boil with the jars in it. When it boils, then start timing it and process for 15 minutes for pints. 20—25 minutes for quarts. The water should reach AT LEAST one inch above the lids in your canner.

Remove the jars with a jar lifter and set the jars on a cooling rack or towel to cool.

Store unopened jars of chow-chow relish in a cool, dark place for up to a year.

I have to tell you, I go to the mailbox each day hoping to hear from you. I'm still waiting. I hope you aren't sick. Maybe you've been busy with the midwife all week and couldn't write. Please let me know. I think about our visit every day. It was such a wunderbar-gut time, eh? And an answer to my prayers for sure. I've been talking with Milo about staying on in the dawdi haus after we're married, and he agrees it would work chust fine. I'll stay on working the farm with him and we'll have a bit of privacy with Rosie in our own little place. Perhaps you'd like to visit up here first, for a longer weekend. I'm still quite amazed and a bit perplexed by what goes on in Rosie's head. She is definitely asking after you. Waerent iss Mamm? I caught her sitting up the other morning in her little bed, talking to her dolly and actually asking her—the dolly—if she knew where you were. Can you beat that?

Well, I'll end here. I really hope you are doing okay. Please let me know soon. I'm sure I'll put this in the mail today and then get a letter from you the very next day, crossing in the mail. Stay well my dearest.

Your bruder in Christ,
Henry

Veronica sat at her sewing machine reading the letter once again. Henry seemed completely oblivious to the effect his previous letter had on her. Here it had turned her world upside down. His opinions on…well…everything: the Church's stand on progress in general, pitting the die-hard conservatives (where he clearly stood) against those that dared to update or modernize their way of life, even in the most miniscule way. But it wasn't that black and white. In reality both 'sides' seriously considered each and every step they took when deciding on church matters, voting in fear and trembling after much prayer and reflection. These things weren't taken lightly. The intention on each side was to live godly lives, pleasing to the Lord in a way that would honor their predecessors who had been divinely guided in leading their flocks. They asked themselves if, in the final tally, had they found something they were willing to die for? Their ancestors had been called to die for their faith.

There are hundreds of testimonies to their sacrifice in the *Martyrs Mirror* first published in Holland in 1660 in Dutch by Thieleman J. van Braght, which documents the stories and testimonies of Christian martyrs, specially Anabaptists. The book includes accounts of the martyrdom of the apostles and the stories of martyrs from previous centuries with beliefs similar to the Anabaptists. Next to the Bible, the *Martyrs Mirror* has historically held the most significant and prominent place in Amish homes.

So, could they say they had found something they were willing to die for? To do so might also mean giving up one's will, not an easy thing for most. Often on a daily basis. But if they found themselves not willing to embrace this road less trod, if not, then who had moved? One minister posed that question only recently: "Who moved? You moved away from *Gott* or Him from you?" Then he proceeded to encourage his sheep to go back to the last time they felt close to Him. What is different now? he asked. He wagered there was more humility in that place they'd left; more submission could bring more peace, too. Also, in that time they weren't arguing over mundane issues, he'd also ventured.

Why can't we chust be happy, living a simple, grateful life? she thought. *We have been given so very much. Why can't we respect each other's views without judgement? Shouldn't we be happy where He has planted us and agree to disagree? Must we turn our lives into one big hairy argument? Lord, please help me here. Dear*

Jesus, please show us the way. Isn't it enough to pray for the ministers the Church has chosen for us and trust their direction in all of this? Must we turn our lives into a full-blown debate, throwing any peace out the window, dividing families, pitting brother against brother? It seems so very judgmental. And here are we not exhorted not to judge? It seems like a whole lot of energy being spent over such mundane trivia. Maybe I am the one who's misguided here. I chust *don't know anymore.*

Feeling utterly deflated, Veronica set this latest missive down by the sewing table. Smoothing out the next seam with both hands she let out a long sigh and began sewing the soft sage-green cloth. Such a small dress and pinafore for Rose wouldn't take long to finish. What will take just as long however is the dolly-size duplicate for Rosemary with such tiny seams and tucks—Rose's much-loved doll.

Veronica had traced around Rosemary on an old sheet of paper taken from a calendar during the visit and whipped up a pattern that she could sew that would fit without the doll actually being present. She planned on making matching clothes for the doll, identical to the other dresses she was planning for Rose, too. What Rose wore on their visit was obviously a hand-me-down, well-worn and also getting a bit tight. Edith shouldn't be expected to keep up with Rose's wardrobe besides all of her own *kinner*, especially now while she was battling morning sickness once again.

This dress was another matter. She'd borrowed Hazel's size four dress pattern from her expansive pattern collection when she was last there. Hazel didn't have grandchildren but had the luxury of more time than most *mamms* or *grossmammis* to sew for the busiest families in the district. She was also often sent two or more little girls on their way to school every morning to braid their hairs. Her little dresses were coveted in the area. Beautifully sewn, they had double hems which could be let down as the child grew. The waists also had an extra tuck designed to be easily let out or mended should some little girl rip it playing baseball at school or climbing up into a hayloft searching out kittens or playing on the outhouse roof during recess, which they were soundly punished for if caught.

Veronica spun the hem around 180 degrees under the needle, let down the presser foot, and ever so slowly proceeded to stitch back just a couple of inches over the hem line to ensure it wouldn't unravel. Clipping the thread with her nippers, she held up the sweet little frock. Then she hugged it to her chest. Of course, that's when the tears erupted once more. They were doing that a lot lately.

Laying the dress down in her lap she collected all the *schnibbles*—the scraps. She sorted them into two piles on the sewing table: scraps too small to save but would still serve for stuffing a teddy bear or toy horse, and those that might be just right for the dolly blanket Veronica had planned to be sent along with the dresses. Next, she counted out the green buttons for the dress and pinafore. She'd have time in the evening to sew those on and finish the dress.

She loved making the miniature quilts. They always sold well at the farmers' markets, too. The women in the community often shared a table, bringing along all sorts of crafts. Hot pads, bowl warmers, aprons, embroidered kitchen towels, half pint jars of jams and pickles and chow-chow, whittled wooden spoons, homemade candy and baked goods, too. She had been only eight when her *mamm* helped her make her first quilt for her own little doll, Cornelia. Then she remembered that she hadn't made any Amish dolls in ages. They took time but it helped pass the long evenings, especially in winter. She mentally added Amish dolls to her list of possible Christmas presents. *Without a house full of* kinner, *I could become a veritable factory,* she mused. At the thought of children, the tears were soon gathering once again. *Though I wouldn't grudge a few in the years to* kumm. *Dear Lord, what do you have planned anyway? Dare I hope? I* chust *wish you would take away the longing so I could get on with my life. Will it never end?*

The hardest mathematics to master is that which allows us to count our blessings.
- Amish saying

CHAPTER 9

Zebras

Back home in Milverton, Ontario, Canada, Henry and his brother Milo were in the barn hitching up the buggy for church Sunday. Yodeling in harmony echoed back to them from the rafters. A tradition that had been passed down from the Swiss-Amish generations ago continued in small enclaves of Amish throughout North America.

"What's she really like?" Milo asked Henry when they'd secured the horse and buggy.

"She's sweet. Not bossy, not flighty, *chust* a nice *frau*. Not too short, sort of like Edith. Not too *geblumpt,* not skinny either. Her hairs are dark, darker than Becky's. She reminds me of our *mamm,* if I am honest. I think gray eyes, not bright blue. I think she is pretty for sure. She's definitely a *gut* cook. She made great *vorrot* and all. She can bake, too. Some things I'd never seen before. The house was real tidy and the garden was for sure *redded* up."

Henry thought another minute as he stood next to the buggy. He waved away a fly before continuing. "She's pretty direct, I'd say. Not gossipy, not real chatty either. Definitely not superficial. No, she's been through too much trouble. It does that to you, for sure. Not shy though. Pretty smart too. She'd been a schoolteacher. We have that in common. I think you'd like her." Then as an afterthought he added, "Rosie sure did. I think if it was up to her, Rosie would have us married like six months ago already," he said chuckling.

Back in the house Edith was going over each child with a comb and a wash rag. A milky mustache or a wild hairdo wouldn't do at all for church. Neither would an unbuttoned shirt, would one of the little *buwe* be having aspirations of growing a few chest hairs to show off should one suddenly appear, finally catching up with the older *bruders*. The *kinner* obediently lined up for the inevitable inspection.

"That'll have to do," Edith finally pronounced, while aiming well and then tossing the rag into the sink from across the kitchen where she sat, the children lined up in front of her. She watched long enough to make sure it hit its mark before jumping up and ducking to see in the tiny mirror by the door if her *kapp* was askew or properly placed. Then she bent over to tie the strings on the bonnet being worn by her almost four-year old niece, Rose, in the end also pronouncing it *gut*.

"Okay, youse all. *Ks!* Go!" she shooed them out as she popped another piece of crystalized ginger candy in her mouth. It was the only thing that saved her most days from the morning sickness. The forty-five-minute drive while being jostled in a hot cramped buggy smelling of barn would not exactly help matters there, though she could always hope.

In the home district where Veronica lived it was also an every-other-week church service. Her drive would be more like twenty-five minutes tops. It was a balmy day which fit with her mood. You couldn't be grumpy out in this beautiful landscape. Every *Amische* farm she passed was ringed by fields of alfalfa, hay, corn or soybeans, the cash crops that supported each household. The families' kitchen gardens were separate, growing by leaps and bounds just now. The rain had done its work and the sun cooperated, too. Flower gardens festooned the homes up to the porches where flower baskets were hung by the front doors. The mules and work horses had the day off too, being Sunday, and were grazing in the paddocks. Sheep, cows, goats, ducks, geese, guinea fowl and chickens, and dogs and cats were wandering over the farms or lolling in the early morning sun. The pigs were usually corralled closer to the main barns. Smart enough to figure out how to escape they were carefully monitored day and night to check that their enclosures would hold. They were hard to catch once they decided to run. Dangerous too. Pig bites are especially nasty. In the Midwestern U.S. more people die of pig bites than of lightning strikes. (Just a bit of trivia Veronica remembered from her reading.)

The next farm she passed as she sipped coffee from her to-go thermos was a carbon copy of the preceding one. But wait! She pulled up on the reins, gulping the coffee and sputtering half of it out, almost choked on it. She couldn't believe what she was seeing. Zebras! And llamas and smaller alpacas. And over...what in the world are those? Emus? Or were they ostriches? She stopped the buggy to inspect this scene better. *What planet am I on?* she thought to herself.

Her horse appeared just as flummoxed as she watched the rare animals also. Then it twigged. She had read about this farm recently, as some Amish were branching out to raise exotic breeds. Humpback Dairies in Missouri had been doing it for years—at least awhile yet—selling camel milk and the much-coveted llama and alpaca wool fleeces.

There are Amish both in Canada and the U.S. now raising buffalo and bison on government grants to encourage the species to come back from the brink of extinction. Even wild boar and elk are harvested annually by Amish farmers to add to the lucrative business. According to a Texas veterinarian the ostrich and emu business in the U.S. (which now includes Amish farms) will soon lead the world in raising ostrich chicks, apparently the next cash crop for their meat in the markets in Europe. Cowboy boots made from ostrich hide are quickly becoming all the rage. A full-grown single mating pair can fetch as much as $35,000.

Finally tearing herself away from the zoo, she resumed her ride to church where she drove in by the large farmhouse and turned the reins over to Benjamin who had come over to park her buggy and lead the horse into the pasture.

She had a hard time concentrating on the sermon that day, still wondering at the strange animals. That was until the second minister began his sermon. The message was clear: It was unequivocally meant for her and her alone. *Gott* had heard her prayers.

He cleared his throat to begin his discourse. Then looking over the heads of the congregation he spoke.

"The callings of a man and woman in marriage are different, yet equal in worth. According to the New Testament, the husband is to be the head of the family, and the wife his helper. He must never dominate her but should cherish and serve her in humility. In some Anabaptist Plain communities, the bridegroom actually promises—he vows—at their wedding to always honor and respect his bride and is reminded of the apostle Peter's warning that if he neglects this, *Gott* may refuse his prayers. Likewise, a wife should support her husband in what is good. Above all, both spouses alike are charged with leading each other closer to Christ."

Veronica was stunned. How could he know of her struggle? But this sermon was explicitly meant for her. It could not be otherwise. There must be others wrestling with these same problems, then, no? There was nothing vague about it. God was indeed very near. Thinking back to the little inspirational calendar sitting on her dresser she whispered the words to herself as she'd only recently read there: "...and He will tell you what to do."

The *frau* sitting next to Veronica silently jabbed her in the ribs with her elbow while gravely frowning, the meaning more than obvious: Do NOT talk during church! The woman on the bench right in front of her turned around and glared at her likewise, her eyebrows sternly pinched, silently admonishing her. Veronica felt her cheeks blushing, embarrassed at her infraction. *Can't do that again,* she thought to herself. *But how can You know? I guess because you are* Gott. *Of course You can do anything, know everything.* She let out a long, measured breath then. *It's for Henry too,* she realized then. *I will have to write to him and tell him. Maybe we actually will find our way forward. I'd practically given up after that last fiasco, that letter.* Just then a bowl of church sugar cookies was passed to her from down the bench, marking the halfway point in the service, designed to keep the little ones distracted until after the last hymn. *Those cookies look mighty* gut, she thought then as she passed the bowl onto her left. *Better not. I'm in enough trouble all ready as it stands,* she sighed, moving the cookies down the row.

And then, as if that wasn't enough to marvel at for one day, right after a hymn which dragged on infernally, the slow way all Plain hymns were sung, the next and final sermon was the icing on the cake, so to speak. She was still thinking about the cookies and how hungry she was getting when his words broke through her daydreaming.

"As you grow in love, you help each other, gently, peacefully, constantly, accepting the weaknesses of each other with deep love and great patience, for that is how the Lord has treated you. Your goal is to become a family, a 'community of love,' accepting all the pain, the problems, the difficulties that every family must go through if it is going to become a community of love."

I don't believe this, she told herself. She continued thinking about it as she headed for the kitchen in the farmhouse to help with the lunch after the final hymn. Then she remembered the text she'd read as she was dressing only this morning. It was from the little inspirational calendar sitting on her dresser. Her spiritual sister, Catherine Doherty coming to her rescue once again.

God speaks quietly, very quietly but He does speak, and He will make known to you what He wants you to do. ~ C. D.

CHAPTER 10

A Mail Order Bride

As she entered the large kitchen to help with setting up lunch after church, she saw Clara standing there as if waiting for her, which was indeed the case. The woman was relentless. Clara had personally taken it upon herself to find Veronica a husband. No amount of reasoning would convince Clara otherwise that Veronica was not interested, thank you very much. Clara saw this as a sacred quest, a divinely inspired, delegated mission from above for which there would be untold blessings should she deliver.

Clara had decided close to seven years ago now, just a few months after the fatal buggy accident that took Veronica's husband, Amos, that she would succeed in finding the perfect match for Veronica. It would take work and the fact that Veronica seemed opposed to the idea all this time made the endeavor even more of a challenge for Clara. Clara thrived on challenges. Not only did she first have to convince Veronica that it was the right thing to do and get her to change her mind, much less agree to it, but she would also have to research the available pool of eligible men which would prove to be quite an undertaking. There were

Amish communities throughout North *and* South America which included all of Canada besides.

Recently Clara had enlisted her cousin Judy for help with the project. Judy lived in Canada. Clara needed maximum support for this venture. She'd need as many troops on the ground as possible. Veronica would be rendered defenseless against these odds, Clara told herself.

Judy was honored to be asked to be a part of this elite group and took her assignment seriously. She couldn't wait to tell her friends at their next quilting meetup. Winter could get mighty long, especially in Canada. Quiltings and other get-togethers helped the *fraus* get through the protracted winters. Amish have long lived in Canada, with roots in the country dating to the 1800s. Today Amish number nearly five thousand souls in Canada, in dozens of communities. Judy had her work cut out for her.

Clara had also recently written to her sister-in-law Linda who lived in Missouri in an Amish community there. That settlement was growing by leaps and bounds. She also knew that New York, Wisconsin, Michigan and Kentucky were equally represented and growing. Texas and Idaho weren't far behind. Linda composed a circular letter which would hopefully supply enough traction to do the job in her small part of the world. She rightly assumed that each of the recipients of the letters would help expand their reach and send them out to others in their circles also. She had considered placing ads in the numerous Amish magazines and newspapers like the *Lady's Journal, The Budget, Single Symphony,* and *Family Life,* but had second thoughts about such a plan. Veronica could very well be offended by such blatant commercialism. A mail order bride. No, it was a good idea, granted but neither Linda, Judy nor Clara would risk completely alienating Veronica, should that one backfire. A mail order bride. On the other hand, they might get some interesting results from that one.

Judy wrote back to Clara as soon as she got the letter.

> *Dear Clara,*
>
> *Greetings in our dear Lord's Name!*
>
> *I think it is a wunderbar-gut idea. Did I ever tell you what I sent into The Budget? Years ago, now? Well, see, our Elmer was still wetting the bed at ten. I felt so sorry for him, but we'd tried everything for it. Vitamin supplements, a little alarm system that woke him at the first sign of dampness. You sewed it into his pajamas. The thing was, though, that when it went off, he and Thaddeus both woke up, practically scared to death, that thing going off like a fire truck, and they both leaped out of bed and both wet all over the floor. They thought that was the funniest thing ever and came to us laughing hysterically.*
>
> *Anyway, I knew he was self-conscious about it, and I tried to reassure him that he would grow out of it eventually. So, I sent in a question to The Budget asking if anyone found a solution for it, and don't ya know, I got dozens and dozens of letters and postcards with all sorts of suggestions. Then one card came all the way from Mexico. I didn't know there were people there, too, who read it, The Budget. Well, so this card came, and they said they'd take him if we didn't want him. Can you believe that? I am still laughing about it as I write this!*
>
> *Anyway, I will see what I can do from my end here. I think it is a gut cause. One of us is sure to snag her a halsband, for certain. And our big news here is that our oldest is getting married in the fall. I will send you an invite. It would be such fun to see you, eh?*
>
> *Love, Judy*

The day after that a letter from Linda arrived.

Dear Clara,
Greetings of love dearest sister in Christ!
I was so glad to get your letter. Here we are hauling in bushels of vegetables and the orchard is ready to pick, too: Apples, two kinds of plums, paw paws and persimmon trees are always wunderbar to have and tasty. I've planted heirloom tomatoes here and there together with sweet potatoes this year. I have radishes, squash—no less than four varieties, serrano peppers, eggplants, and cucumbers besides. I have not had much success with corn, but the peas, green beans, pumpkins, melons, bell peppers, and strawberries, well I end up giving away more than I can ever get to freeze or can. It's a bit overwhelming this time of year. Want to kumm down here and have a canning frolic? I could sure put you to work.
I will see what I can do for you in the halsband department. I'll see lots of my friends in the next few weeks, either at church or a baby shower and such. Oh, and we have a school auction kumming up here. We'll get the word out there either way. Wouldn't that be nice to find someone for her?
Your BFF,
Linda

As Veronica washed her hands at the kitchen sink so that she could help with the lunch preparations Clara sidled up to Veronica, her pasted on smile more than obvious. *She should have been an actress,* Veronica thought to herself. *Now behave, you,* she chided herself. *Beheef dich. At least be kind.*

"Why, Veronica. I am so glad to see ya. I am always happy to see ya getting out, not that you are at home feeling sorry for yourself mind you, but it's *chust* healthy to mingle with others."

"I think I mingle plenty, Clara," Veronica answered wryly. "How are you? And your *kinner?* That little one starting school in the fall, is it?" she asked, hoping to derail the conversation as soon as possible and move on to other subjects.

"Yes," Clara answered almost too quickly before moving on to what she was bursting to ask. "Is it a rumor I heard, or is there any truth in it, what they were saying at Millie's Mercantile the other day, that you've had a male caller recently? Maybe it was *chust* a bit of gossip?" Clara was dying to know. This was definitely big news, should it turn out to be true.

"Well, we shouldn't gossip, *ya* know," Veronica instructed Clara. "It never ends well, eh?" Veronica knew this wouldn't put Clara off, really, but it was worth a try.

"But is it true? Where's the *bruder* from?" Clara forged on.

Determined not to open Pandora's box here, at this time, Veronica carefully weighed her words. "Well, time will tell." That was all Veronica decided she would offer her.

"So, it is true then?" Clara asked, instantly animated and holding her breath.

"Where's he from? Are you still writing to him? Have you set a date then?" Clara forged on.

"Time will tell," was all Veronica would offer Clara. At that her jaw was set. She would not give in. Her message was clear: Mind your own business. But as far as Clara was concerned this was the news of the century.

"Aw, come on. I'm your dearest cousin. Can't ya tell me *chust* a little? Huh?" Clara whined.

"Nope," was all Veronica answered as she dried her hands and turned to go help with lunch. Hoping not to sound too unkind, she did offer the woman one tiny morsel: "I will keep you posted though."

But that was not good enough for Clara. Not in the least.

"*Chust* tell me where he's from. Who connected you two?" Clara pressed on.

Veronica pasted on her own best smile and walked away toward Roseanna who was delegating the jobs yet to be covered. Veronica was assigned an enormous, iced sheet cake to cut and place on the little dessert plates stacked there. All one hundred and fifty of them. "Okay, a rectangular pan," she mumbled to herself. "Ten pieces wide by what length? Fifteen? Is that right?" she began mentally scoring the cake into blocks. "That looks *gut*," she said to herself as she cut into the cake. *Yummy. Looks like that Double Chocolate Beet Cake,* she thought to herself as she scraped a good-sized dollop off the knife with a finger and popped it into her mouth. *Yup, that's the best ever* she confirmed. *Yumm!*

We cannot become what we need to be by remaining what we are.
- An Amish teacher's ponderings

CHAPTER 11

No Rest For The Wicked

Dear Kitty, Veronica began to write in her journal. She had been neglecting it for days now. So very discouraged, actually shocked when she received Henry's letter outlining his grudges with the more progressive or forward-thinking members of the Amish churches, almost assuming she would agree with each point contained there. Further, it looked like he thought they should live in Canada, shaking the dust from their feet in the U.S. and their insubordinate brethren there.

None of this had come up during his visit to her home earlier that month. Everything appeared to be more than perfect while he and Rose were there. They'd both felt completely united and felt that God had indeed, miraculously led them together. But now this.

I can't imagine how Gott *will fix this one,* she began to write in her journal. *Why did I ever even hope that things would turn out? It all seemed perfect when he was here. Was it all too much to ask for? To hope? I don't have the faintest clue what to do now. I've shared the letter with a few close to me, like Pennelope and Ruth. They are chust as speechless as I am. Flummoxed.*

Ferhoodled. So, do I chust pray and trust? What do I do if he shows up back here? What do I write? How long can I ignore the letter? I can't lie or tell him I am having second thoughts, can I? It would break his heart. Never mind that his letter practically broke mine. Actually not 'practically.' It chust about did. I guess that is all I can do, pray and wait. Wait and pray. Gott *sure has His work cut out for Him with this one....*

I know I can't chust agree with him for the sake of peace. Make myself the martyr and make believe it will all be fine, or it won't kumm between you. Swallow the whole package and pretend for all the years to kumm that it doesn't matter. Chust play the submissive wife and let him think he has got it all right. Is that even honest? What does that do to a person, keeping it all inside until it bursts? Or can you find a way to live with that? Can you really love someone unconditionally with all your heart while your mind has its reservations? Veronica put down the pencil and closed the notebook.

She got up from the table with a groan then and looked around the kitchen. She tried to summon up the conundrums from the past, all those issues that had been discussed right here, fought through at this very table, though she wasn't privy to everything. What had these walls witnessed? Or heard? If only the walls could talk. How many times had they all sat around this table and worked out so many of life's puzzles? They always seemed to find a way. Was marriage supposed to be this hard? Why had her own parents apparently escaped such division? Or had they? Did they shield their children from it so well they didn't have a clue about all the things the parents had wrestled with over the years? Had they *chust* waited until the *kinner* were asleep to forge into the other questions too intimate or private for tiny ears? *Mamm* and *Dat* would know what she should do. *They were so wise. But they aren't here....*

Oh! But Aunt Wanda is, she recalled, shocked at her own stupidity. Surely, she of all people would know what to do. A veritable vessel of wisdom and tenderness, honed by years of adversity, suffering, and all that life could throw at you. Purified by fire. Unshakable. That is how Veronica thought of her dear grandmother who had outlived most of her generation. At least in her eighties by now, closer to ninety, anyone would be hard pressed to believe that if you looked at her. Still attending every quilting, every *frolic*, watching the grandbabies; still baking and cooking the best time-honored recipes, still driving her own horse and buggy, oblivious to the years marching on, acting as if she was exempt from the whole entire aging process.

"Time to visit Auntie," Veronica stated simply, to herself. Just the thought gave her courage to face the new day.

"I'll finish my chores first. Then I can take off. *Kaffi*. This calls for *kaffi*," she told herself, now smiling as she hurried barefoot to the wood stove to pour a mug before going up to the bedrooms. The old stairs creaked as she went up. She was happy to think she might finally be closer to a solution than she'd been in days. It gave her hope. Hope--something she'd been devoid of even in the littlest shred lately. Well, at least since the letter came.

Dressing quickly, she then loitered by the mirror on her dresser to fix her hairs. As she brushed them all out, she again looked at the little calendar there and read the day's offering:

God speaks quietly, very quietly but He does speak, and He will make known to you what He wants you to do.

Well, she thought to herself after a minute. *It* chust

doesn't tell you when or how He'll let you know. But if that's all I got, I'll take it.

Just then the little pager that Midwife Ruth had given her sent up an earsplitting squeal from its hiding place in her purse hanging behind the bedroom door along with a clean dress. Veronica startled at the sound. Then she grabbed the purse and removed the offender. The message on the screen read, "See you soon."

Addressing the little black box, she asked aloud, "Now? Are you kidding me? Really? *Really?* Well, then, I guess *bobbeli* don't ask us when it is convenient now, do they? They *kumm* in their own *gut* time. I wonder who it is?" And with that she shrugged out of the dress she had just put on, the one she wore the day before, but it was not really dirty, good enough for everyday and changed into the clean outfit hanging behind the door. "No rest for the wicked," she concluded before racing downstairs, juggling the half-full coffee mug, while clipping on her *kapp* with her other hand to meet the van.

It wasn't straight, the *kapp,* but there were worse things in the world. You never knew if a baby would wait for you to arrive. Veronica remembered then that that they shared a good saying from one of the midwives she knew, a retired midwife who had been in the trenches for decades, so to speak. She had said, "We are in the business of mortality, its beginning and sometimes at its end. We are midwives. We are tired for the better part of our careers. That is nothing new. We will sleep when we are dead."

"We're probably going to have a long night of it with this one," Ruth informed Veronica after she was settled in the van. "It's her first and those usually take a while, but you never know. I am usually surprised when I think I know what to expect."

"Who is it?" Veronica wanted to know. This would be her third birth as Midwife Ruth's assistant—or apprentice—whatever she was supposed to be. Truth be told she had no idea what she was doing even agreeing to help Ruth who assured Veronica she was the perfect person for the job. Ruth continued filling Veronica in on the case.

"It's Joel and Dora. They're both *chust* nineteen. Pretty young but obviously hard working and doing well. I love delivering first babies," Ruth gushed.

"They have no idea what to expect, so they are pretty clueless usually, which has its benefits. They aren't worried about anything much, don't have expectations or want to control it all. They're usually quite trusting and *chust* go along with whatever you say. Some are scared, and that's usually their own *mamm's* fault or some auntie or sister who's been spreading horror stories about their own births. I wish they wouldn't do that. It for sure doesn't help. Ever. Telling the girl her own labor was forty-eight hours long. They don't even know what they're talking about.

"Anyway, we don't count pre-labor, when you *chust* have practice contractions and they *kumm* and go, and they think they are unbearable and have no idea what is going on. Pre-labor doesn't count. I tell them that, but they aren't convinced. It hasn't really become hard labor yet. When the contractions are five minutes apart and the water has broken spontaneously, that's when you can call it labor. It isn't even stage one till then. The hospital would send them home at that point, till it's real, and they are all disappointed and start walking all the country roads thinking it will 'turn it on' and by the time they call you again they're too tuckered out for the real thing.

I usually tell them to go back home, if they aren't there

already, and eat something like a whole stack of pancakes, smothered in butter and syrup, build up their strength and take a nap. That's the best thing they can do. Most will do it, but then there are always the ones who want to get things revved up and *chust* keep walking. Well, we'll see what Judith and Joel have in mind soon enough."

When they arrived, Joel stabled Ruth's horse and Veronica grabbed the box of supplies from the back of the buggy. Ruth explained on the way up to the back door that this was the second box of supplies. "I delivered the first box last week. All the clean towels, Chux pads to cover the bed, the cord clamping supplies all wrapped up and sterilized."

"So what is left then in this box?" Veronica wanted to know.

"The meds I am allowed to carry, like Pitocin. It's for bleeding when I can't get the uterus to contract enough after the birth using massage only," she explained. "And the scales, the suctioning equipment, that kind of stuff, and this other case is oxygen if the baby needs it."

"Yikes!" Veronica squeaked as she stopped dead in her tracks on the way to the house.

"They are pretty routine events but if we see anything we can't manage we'll call for proper backup. EMTs and an ambulance," Ruth stopped walking too and explained.

"Gosh. How often do you need to do that?" Veronica wanted to know.

"I've never been to a birth by myself that we had to transfer. Usually some sign—a red flag--will pop up during the earliest part of labor or your late prenatal checkups. Then we'll plan a hospital birth and switch gears. Sometimes the doctor will meet us at the hospital and get everything back on track. They usually let us stay and work with them.

"There was one birth at the clinic last year that did need intervention, though. Everything went really well, the birth and the *mamm*, no problems there. I was discharging her about six hours after the birth, puttering around the clinic, washing the sheets, autoclaving—sterilizing—the instruments. I was alone with one of the doulas who was going to go home with her and settle her there. It was their second baby. A boy. Good weight and all. Everyone else had left the clinic. It was pretty late.

"All of a sudden, I went over to the baby—the *mamm* was sleeping—and I wasn't too sure about the baby's color. I picked him up and could feel he was floppy, not normal muscle tone even for a sleeping *bobbel*. I knew this didn't look right. I wasn't sure what exactly it was but got out the oxygen and gave him a bit which didn't seem to help him pink up at all. So I called the clinic supervisor who told me to call the city's closest Children's Hospital and relayed what was going on. I had *chust* certified for the NRP neonatal resuscitation course which gave me enough to know what to do or when to start CPR. Boy, but were they fast. They must have driven one hundred miles an hour. All of a sudden there were doctors in the room, pediatricians and ICU nurses. They got an umbilical IV going and they brought in this...this thing.

"It looked like a spaceship. It was like a miniature rocket on wheels with an incubator in the middle where they do whatever they needed to, even operate, right there. The air and temperature are all regulated for the baby. So we packed up the *mamm* and headed over to the hospital following the ambulance.

"Everyone was so very kind. I didn't tell the *mamm* then, but I did tell the supervisor that the baby also gave me the impression of possibly having Downs. Just his features and some markers like hyperextended toes and Simion lines on his palms, though only blood tests could give them a definitive diagnosis. I knew that Downs babies tend to have more incidents of heart and diaphragm defects, though not all. One newborn in every seven hundred births could have Downs. They are also at a higher risk of hearing loss, anemia, and problems with metabolism. That comes out to about 6,000 babies being born each year in the U.S. with Downs."

"I had no idea," Veronica said shaking her head. "Was he okay in the end?"

"He was wonderful. He had a heart murmur that they could fix. I saw him a couple of years later, the happiest little guy on earth. He was absolutely darling," Ruth said.

They hung up their shawls and left their shoes by the mat at the back door. There were two *grossmammis* there already who could report to Ruth.

"I'm so glad you're here! I don't think the waters have broken," the first grandmother said.

Then the second grandmother explained, "she was feeling poorly about noon so I came over and made them some lunch. Dora is in there resting now. She's had a few pains, but nothing close. And she's drinking juices and tea and going to the outhouse regularly. She's about a week late, *eh?*"

"Something like that," Ruth agreed as she set out the boxes on the kitchen table.

Dora wandered into the kitchen then, barefoot, in her flannel nightie, woken by the visitors coming in. She rubbed her eyes before focusing on the guests there.

"Oh, Ruth! Thank you for *kumming*. I was starting to think this one didn't wanna get born," Dora said, chuckling.

"I told your *bobbel* last week when I saw you that I was

giving him his eviction notice if I hadn't been called by the end of this week," Ruth laughed.

"How would you do that?" Veronica asked.

"Castor oil is often effective in inducing labor," Ruth whispered to Veronica behind her hand. "I also had one *mamm* got on a bike and went on a long ride on a bumpy dirt road. It worked, actually. My own *mamm* swore that the old *Amische* wives' tale worked every time, too."

"What was that?" Veonica asked.

"She said you *chust* go visiting a friend and it will start. She said it worked for her, every time," Ruth explained nodding her head.

The first grandma was at the kitchen counter dividing up a sweet potato pie. The other one was bouncing on the huge birth ball that Ruth had brought the week before. The birth ball was recently added to labor wards around the world with the rationale that staying upright, and bouncing would help the baby engage in the pelvis completely, thus shortening labor in many cases.

"Anyone want a little midnight *nachen?* I brought *bief.* It's sweet potato. Any takers?" she asked, popping open a tub of whipped cream. The granny arranged the snack around the supplies strewn across the old oak table. The *kaffi* was put on the wood stove and mugs brought out. The granny on the birth ball was rocking back and forth on it now, her bare feet slapping the wood floor every time she rolled forward on it. She resumed gently bouncing up and down while sipping her coffee.

"Well, is this ever nice?" the granny asked while handing Dora the first generous slice. As she stood up and reached across the table, which was not done easily with such a large belly in the way, they all heard an audible POP! Everyone froze. Veronica looked at Ruth who looked at Dora, who took in the grandmothers' surprised looks evidenced by their raised eyebrows. The birth ball stilled. Finally, one of them spoke.

"What was that?" she demanded.

Joel wandered into the kitchen just then. He had been dozing in the bedroom, oblivious to the recent developments.

Dora answered the question on everyone's mind.

"My water *chust* broke!" she declared, chuckling while surveying the growing puddle forming at her feet. "What do I do now?" she asked.

"Well, you go ahead and eat that. You'll be needing it!" Ruth ordered, grabbing a few towels from the stack in the box. At the same time, she noted the color of the amniotic fluid. It was clear, which meant a happy baby that wasn't feeling stressed. She made a mental note to add this information into the chart. Checking the clock on the wall she read the time there.

"Will I get contractions now?" Dora wanted to know.

The granny on the birth ball resumed bouncing. As she stretched out one hand to return her mug to the table, she lost her balance and rolled over onto the floor, the giant lime green ball spinning off into the corner of the kitchen. She landed on her back, feet in the air, skirts fluttering as she went down. Her *kapp* flew off and the bun at the back of her head exploded apart, sending hair pins skittering across the floor. Horrified at such an indignity, she laughed out loud at the absurdity of it all just the same.

"You might," Ruth answered Dora when she stopped laughing at the spectacle. "It could be a while too. We're not in a hurry here."

Joel just stood looking at all those assembled there. Finally, he asked rather shyly, "Anything goin' on?"

Dora filled him in as he sat in the chair the grandmother passing out the pie indicated for him, setting down a large slice of pie adorned with a generous dollop of whipped cream in front of him with her other hand. He obediently picked up the fork there and dug into it. They visited around the table for another hour. Ruth suggested that Dora try to catch a nap while things seemed to slow down. Ruth followed her into the bedroom bringing along the little hand-held Doppler. They could listen to the baby at each stage with it. He sounded great so far. Dora finished her pie and handed the plate and fork back to Ruth.

"Try to nap," Ruth encouraged her as she followed Dora back into the bedroom. "I predict by morning you'll have that baby in your arms," she added while pulling up the quilt and tucking it in around her.

"And at your age..." the one grandmother whispered through gritted teeth as she helped the other *grossmammi* up from the floor.

While Dora and Joel dozed off back in the bedroom after being completely stuffed with pie, the grandmothers tidied up the kitchen and settled on the couch in the great room to visit quietly there, the one promising to stay away from birth balls.

Ruth opened the chart and made some notes while pointing out everything there for Veronica's edification. It was again time to check Dora's blood pressure. Tip toeing into the bedroom Ruth gently stroked Dora's arm while whispering, "I *chust* need to check your blood pressure. You can go back to sleep then, dear."

Going out of the room quietly, Ruth waved Veronica over to the table.

"Her blood pressure is a tad higher than to my liking," she whispered.

"What can you do for that?" Veronica asked frowning, the first hiccup so far.

"At this point we'll *chust* watch it carefully. Very carefully," Ruth explained. "My protocols state that if it is even one degree over 140 over 80 that we transfer or call the doctor on call and get his input."

"Why is that bad then?" Veronica wanted to know.

"It can be the first sign of a problem called 'pre-eclampsia,'" Ruth said quietly while noting this in the chart. "We don't wait until we are in hot water with this one. We'll watch it a bit, checking every fifteen minutes and then re-think our direction depending on where it is."

"Are you worried?" Veronica asked.

"I am concerned. We must follow protocols, though. If we fudge on any of that we'll lose all credibility with the wider medical community, thinking we can manage it, going in all confident thinking we know better, that we have that training. In actual fact, it is outside of our scope of practice, along with multiple *bobbeli*—twins, breech births, and things like a face or shoulder presentation. One of my mentors when I started told me that you can't go into this work without humility *and* respect. It is *chust* too awesome a responsibility."

Veronica thought about that for a moment. "You're right," she breathed out, nodding while considering that.

While Ruth was busy with the charting, and the grannies were chatting quietly on the couch, Veronica served seconds on coffee to all there. Placing the pot back on the wood stove, she came and sat near Ruth again. Opening her sewing bag, she pulled out the little Tumbling Blocks quilt she was working on, telling Ruth that it was for Rose's doll. It was all pieced and just needed to be hand quilted now. She had begun stitching little hearts in the blocks in the four corners.

"You really are going ahead with this wedding then, aren't ya?" Ruth asked.

"Well," Veronica began with a deep sigh. "I've kind of, like, sort of bumped into a wall there."

"How so?" Ruth stopped writing and looked at Veronica.

"...more like the Empire State Building. It's a long story..." she began, "but I guess we have time now."

"I'm listening," Ruth said. Veronica stood up and walked over to her purse hanging on a peg by the back kitchen door. She retrieved the letter and returning, handed it to Ruth.

Pushing her glasses up her nose a tad and taking a long drink of the tepid coffee in the mug by the charts, Ruth began to read.

Veronica got up and grabbing the mugs off the table went over to the sink, dumping the old coffee out. She started a new pot, checking the fire box and freshening it up with sticks from the tinder box by the stove. After a minute had passed, when the kindling took, she added a small log. The coffee would take no time now to perk.

Ruth looked up from the letter then. "You're not kidding me, eh? Where did this *kumm* from anyway? The moon?" Veronica only nodded, shook her head and then fished for a hankie in her pocket. Ruth finished the first page and excused herself to check on Dora. Seating herself back at the table when she returned, she continued reading. Then carefully folding it up, handed it back to Veronica.

"I see," she said. "And you didn't have a clue while he was here?"

"No," Veronica said. "I can't even write back. It's been two weeks. He's gonna think I fell off the face of the earth. What if he takes it into his head to *chust* show up back here? I couldn't bear it. I'm so *ferhooodled,* Ruth. I wish I'd never started this whole courting thing. Why didn't I know better? How could I let this happen? And ya know, I never asked for baptism and joined church to defend outhouses out in the yard over indoor ones."

"Well," Ruth began slowly. "You didn't know. You couldn't tell him where you stand, like in a letter? Straight speaking like the ministers tell us. Let him know what you think. Let him know what you find hard...if you think you two can salvage the relationship or if it is a dead-end street. Honesty is the only way I can see. I'm so sorry Veronica. You've been through so much. It really seemed like a miracle at the beginning, finding one another."

"Oh, I know. Maybe I should write the letter. I'll pray about it. And I'll let you know, I promise," Veronica told Ruth while daubing her eyes with her handkerchief.

Even if you are on the right track, you might get run over if you just sit there.
- Amish saying

CHAPTER 12

Blowing Raspberries

One of the grandmothers picked up *The Budget* newspaper that was sitting on the couch between them. While she was perusing the contents page, she mentioned to the other grandmother that she was looking for the 'Accidents and Fires' page that listed those things throughout the Amish world.

"Here it is," she finally announced. "Now I saw this at home and wanted to ask you Anastasia," she said, "You've got family back in Pennsylvania, don't ya?"

Anastasia's eyes were closed as she was dozing off. Sitting up, she blinked and shook herself awake, her eyes flying open at the mention of her name.

"Ya," she answered, still blinking.

"Well, here it is," she announced. "You've got Byler relations in the Dayton area, don't cha?" she repeated. Anastasia nodded.

"Well, it says here," she began to read. "'That a someone...ah, Byler had a mishap at work and cut off his left hand at the wrist when he was trying to get part of a board out of a cut off saw. I don't know what he will do to keep occupied now as he works at a pallet shop a mile from home,' it says here. Well, I know what he'll be doing," Elizabeth added, shuddering at the very idea of such an accident. "He'll be recovering from that for the next year!"

"Yikes!" Anastasia responded. "Elizabeth, that's awful! Those poor people!"

"Here's another one. From Missouri," she read. "'Jessie, twenty years old, fell off the roof of a house they were fixing. He stepped on a piece of tin that hadn't been fastened. It slid and took him for a quite a ride. He is not paralyzed, but very sore.' That is one lucky kid, eh?" Both grandmothers nodded in agreement to that.

Ruth was checking the baby again with the Dopler. He still sounded really happy.

"Your baby's heart rate is great. It is still around one-hundred and sixty beats a minute. Girls usually have higher heart beats like that. Boys are usually closer to the one-hundred-forties. You don't know what you're having yet, do you?" Ruth inquired. Joel answered for Dora who was now slowly breathing through a contraction, her eyes closed and eyebrows frowning in intense concentration.

"No, we wanted it to be a surprise," Joel offered. Then, "So how is she doing? Does it always take this long?" he wanted to know.

Ruth explained, "She is doing great. Babies *kumm* when they're ready though. It can be slow or speed up at any time. I'm going to check her blood pressure again in a few minutes. I'll let you know if anything changes."

Satisfied with her answer he wandered back into the bedroom and lay down next to Dora, thinking he would rest for now. Going back to the kitchen table Ruth finished off her pie and coffee. Then she stood up and stretched, the look of concern obvious.

Addressing Veronica she explained. "Well, things seem

to be going in the right direction, but her blood pressure is still on the top end of normal. I am thinking we should consider some way to get it down soon or we'll have to transfer to the hospital where the doctor can give her some meds to bring it down and monitor it better. We don't want to wait for it to go any higher at this point. I'm going to go talk to the *grossmammis* and let Dora rest. We'll see what we should do then," Ruth explained.

The two grandmothers were still visiting in the great room, tittering over tidbits in *The Budget*. Ruth sat down in the bent wood hickory rocking chair across from them.

She cleared her throat to get their attention.

"I think we need to be a bit concerned about Dora's blood pressure. If we can't get it down, I am afraid we will need to go to the hospital. It could turn into something more serious, and I won't risk that. What I am thinking is that we can try some natural things to fix it first. That may or may not work." She let that thought settle in.

Elizabeth spoke up first. "What can you do, then?" she asked, instantly worried at this new development. "What complications are you talking about?"

"Well, it's called pre-eclampsia. That can be very serious. I've heard that garlic actually brings down blood pressure. If that doesn't work in the first hour, I think it isn't going to be our answer, but I'd like to try it. Do either of you have any garlic supplements or vitamins at home?"

Annastasia was instantly energized and wanted to help. "Our house is *chust* next door," she said, popping up from the sofa. "I'll see what I've got. Ya know, I have that little room that's my store in the back of the house. They're always *kumming* by to pick up different pills."

Ruth was very grateful. This could really help. She said a quick prayer that it would.

The grandma slipped on her Crocks at the kitchen door

and grabbing a flashlight set out. Ruth went in to see Dora then. Things were slowly picking up. The contractions weren't yet five minutes apart, but she knew she could guess that Dora's cervix was dilating at about one centimeter per hour. This was definitely passing into the first or active stage of labor. Ruth knew too frequent checks for precise dilation often slowed down labor. She already knew the baby's head was engaged in the pelvis properly by just 'walking' her fingers along Dora's stomach and discerning his position.

The Doppler told her that Baby was quite content, and the contractions were not causing him (or her) any stress at this point. If they were and Baby's heart rate went up significantly (Tachycardia) with contractions and then slowed as the contraction ebbed away, or that the heart rate went way down (Bradycardia) during a contraction and did not recover when it passed, then he might not be coping with the stress of labor at that point. Even one reading of under fifty to ninety beats per minute that didn't recover quickly would be considered a red flag.

When Anastasia returned with the garlic pills, Ruth explained the idea to Dora who was happy to comply. "You may end up smelling like garlic for a week after, I gotta warn ya," Ruth told her, chuckling as she poured out the pills into her hand. "But let's give this a go, okay?"

Dora nodded and took the glass of juice that her *grossmammi* offered. Twenty minutes later when Ruth checked Dora's blood pressure it had dropped into a better range already. It had worked. Brilliantly. She wasn't worried either that it had been eight hours since Dora's bag of waters broke. Leaving out the internal exams actually helped by not introducing any germs into the cervix.

Dora's temperature had also stayed perfectly normal through the night so far. Ruth carefully charted all of this in her notes pointing out her rationale to Veronica as she wrote. "Many hospitals and doctors worry and begin counting the hours after the water breaks and rush to induce labor artificially at that point, but some studies have proven that even at seventy-two hours, the second or pushing stage, usually starts spontaneously. To instruct a mother to push too soon can cause swelling of the cervix and can make a vaginal birth impossible, necessitating a C-section."

"The other thing you can do" Ruth explained to Dora, "is to breathe out the contraction. When you hold your breath or keep it all inside and don't make a sound, it kind of isn't released and you are slowing things down. One of my mentors when I was training, Ina May Gaskin, one of the first midwives in the U.S. to publish her own findings, always said that when your throat and neck and jaw are loose, then you can't but *not* keep everything down below loose too. Try blowing out like a horse—it's called 'blowing raspberries' actually—like this, letting your lips go really loose when you blow," Ruth demonstrated. The two *mammis* were in the bedroom by now and they too were trying to blow raspberries. Joel couldn't believe what he was seeing. His eyebrows could not have risen any higher and he sat there with his mouth open. Ruth and the *mammis* dissolved into spasms of giggles over this new idea. Dora laughed out loud and couldn't stop giggling even when the next contraction revved up.

"Ina May also said laughing or singing through labor can help you relax and open up," Ruth added.

So, raspberries it was. Ruth had Dora visit the outhouse once more, noticing that when Dora got out of bed, the contractions went up in intensity. When they got back from the outhouse, Ruth suggested that Joel and Dora go out, breathe the fresh air and walk around the farm for an hour or so. It was a stunningly, beautiful, balmy night with a full moon besides. No one else would be about and the horses in the paddock wouldn't care that Dora was in her nightie.

Good character, like good soup is usually homemade.
- Amish saying

Part Two

Don't pray for rain if you are going to complain about the mud.
- Amish saying

CHAPTER 13
Rhinoceros and Elephants

The grannies took this break to tidy up the bedroom and make up the sheets with a clean rubber sheet underneath covered by a draw sheet. The coffee mugs and pie plates were all collected, and Ruth opened a clean towel on the top of the dresser and showed Veronica the items she was laying out there that she might need to ask for.

"What are the scissors for?" Veronica wanted to know.

"It is very rare, especially if we don't rush the pushing stage, to have to do what's called an episiotomy. I've actually only seen it once. Most of our midwives use hot compresses on the perineum to help it stretch along with almond oil. Our thinking too, is that small tears can be stitched quite easily, but an episiotomy that extends into muscle tissue takes much longer to heal, causes scarring and is generally overused in hospitals. I'll also need the scissors to cut the cord, but if it's around the baby's neck too tight to slip over the head at that point, we might need to clamp and cut it before the shoulders *kumm* out. Again, pretty rare but we're prepared."

Veronica stood up and brought her coffee mug to the

stove. Truth be told, she'd heard enough details—more than she needed to hear—and didn't have the stomach for much more.

"Now I know why I'm not a nurse or a midwife," Veronica directed this observation at Ruth, shaking her head.

"You get used to it, really," Ruth said.

"I don't know if I ever will," Veronica shot back. "I was wondering, by the way, have you met that Amish nurse over in the next district? Phoebe something? They say it's been a huge help to the community. All sorts of things."

"I think you should shadow her for a couple of weeks. It would be super interesting, eh?" Ruth suggested. "Yeah, I've met her. She comes in once a week or so and talks with the midwives and the staff about all sorts, things she seen. We love hearing her take on things and giving her feedback."

Just then the kitchen door flew open bringing in a gust of cold air smelling of the farm and the animals.

Joel spoke for Dora then. "This is getting too intense to walk now," he stated as Dora doubled over in the doorway, and then remembered to blow strawberries. Or...what was it...blueberries or raspberries? She couldn't remember which and looked up at Ruth with a painful sort of smile. "Oh, help! I don't know what to do..." she squeaked, her pupils dilated.

"Ina May told me once that when you are getting close, really close, all the blood from your brain leaves there to concentrate on everything down below. Let's *chust* get you comfortable, okay?" Ruth gently guided her to the bedroom after Dora kicked off her slippers on the mat.

The *mammis* followed Dora and Ruth and Joel with Veronica close behind. Ruth silently directed the grandmothers with her hand to the farthest corner of the little room to give her space at the bedside. Ruth sat on the end of the bed then, gently messaging Dora's calf muscles and slowly massaging her feet. It was all quiet. Dora appeared to actually fall into a deep sleep between contractions, deep enough to snore, which seemed amazing to Veronica.

"She's working really hard now," Ruth whispered to Veronica. "We're close. Bring the towels and the almond oil, please." Veronica did exactly as she was told, still puzzling however, how someone could be 'working really hard' while snoring. She decided to ask Ruth about that one later.

Dora was propped up in bed. Joel had been assigned to the head of the bed and instructed how to gently wipe Dora's brow and neck between contractions with a cool cloth. In his other hand he held a tall glass of water for her.

The grannies were silently standing at their post in the corner of the room, quietly blowing raspberries intermittently along with Dora. Veronica sat in a chair beside the dresser with Ruth's supplies laid out should she need anything. The room was completely silent. The dawn just beginning to break could be seen outside the window there. The curtains had been pulled back to let in the morning breeze. Then a woodcock off in the woods somewhere nearby started his annual mating call, beeping and hooting for all he was worth. Ruth smiled at Veronica. The grandmothers had heard it too.

Just then Dora's eyes popped open, and she took a deep breath and held it, looking straight at Ruth. Ruth nodded ever so slightly back and smiled. She was giving Dora permission to push, though the others weren't privy to this sacred unspoken language. All of the animal kingdom and not just humans were born knowing this. No one had to teach Dora how to do this.

That famous midwife, Ina May Gaskin once said it perfectly: "The Creator is not a careless mechanic. Human female bodies have the same potential to give birth as well as aardvarks, lions, rhinoceros, elephants, moose, and water buffalo. Even if it has not been your habit throughout your life so far, I recommend that you learn to think positively about your body."

Ruth knew this too. Dora let out a long breath and took in an even deeper one. Then, tipping her head forward until her chin touched her chest, she pushed while keeping her eyes riveted on Ruth. Ruth held out a hand toward Veronica and whispered, "almond oil" which Veronica dribbled into Ruth's palm just in time for Ruth to cup the little head as it slowly emerged.

"He'll be born on the next contraction. Just rest for a minute," Ruth quietly instructed Dora. The room was again silent. Everyone was holding their breath.

And then her baby was born. Veronica draped a dry receiving blanket over the baby while Ruth lifted the chunky little dishwasher onto Dora's chest. Dora couldn't speak, having just witnessed this most holy of miracles.

"He's here?" Dora asked, still incredulous that it was over.

Ruth nodded, smiling. Then Veronica switched out another dry receiving blanket over the baby, tossing the damp one onto the growing pile of laundry by the bedroom door, while Ruth passed the scissors to Joel who registered absolute panic at the thought that he needed to participate in any way at this point. Ruth clamped the cord when it stopped pulsing and pointed to the segment where Joel should cut it. Then Ruth announced, "And now she's free!"

The grandmothers immediately migrated to the bedside, both talking at once. Ruth concentrated on delivering the placenta into a stainless-steel bowl which would be buried later under the eaves of the house according to Amish tradition. Dora patted the place on the mattress next to her indicating where Joel could settle. They were both still in shock. Soon everyone left the bedroom, giving the new parents time with their precious little one, who really wasn't very little. Later that morning Ruth wrapped the baby in a large cloth diaper knotted at the top and hung the diaper from the fish scale she'd brought in her birthing kit.

"I knew she was big, but not this big," Ruth marveled before pronouncing, "nine pounds, ten ounces!" She really was a beautiful baby with rose-red lips that puckered into a little heart shape. She had a dimple in both cheeks and tiny brown curls.

The grandmothers quickly made themselves useful and put together a wonderful breakfast for everyone, first bringing a tray into the new parents and their little Doreen.

Mother: "Do you know why is breastfeeding so gut?"
Daughter: "I dunno. Why?"
Mother: "Well my mama told me 'cause it's always warm, it's always ready, and it's up high where the cats can't get it!"

- Quaker saying

CHAPTER 14
Plastic Daisies

Ruth and Veronica waited for the van that had brought them to Joel and Dora's farm the day before. The grandmothers stayed behind to help the new parents. Anastasia had gone to the phone booth between the farms that the Amish families had installed for the district's use and called the driver back.

"Let's get together tomorrow to finish up the charting. I'm really spent," Ruth suggested.

"*Gut* idea," Veronica agreed sleepily as they fell into the back seat of the sedan. They got dropped off at their respective houses and both headed for bed, dropping purses, shoes, *kapps*, shawls, and socks along the way to the upstairs. First babies often take longer to come, and Dora's was no exception.

Before she collapsed into bed, Veronica knelt by her bed to pray.

Denki Gott *for everything. A healthy* mamm *and* bobbel, *Ruth's learning, for this new little family. For letting me witness these miracles. My but this isn't anything I could have imagined. Ever. Denki. And please bless Henry and Rose and help me write that letter. It will be a relief to send it and then move on.* Chust *to have an uncomplicated life again. Dear Lord, I am too old for all this drama. Please help....*

At a loss for any more words, she stood up and crawled under the heavy quilt. Her eyes were already closed. Her last thoughts were a prayer of thanksgiving...*for this bed, for food, for how you care for each one of us. For new* bobbeli. *Amen.*

And write that letter she did. Well, she started it. Sitting at the breakfast table the next morning she composed her thoughts over hot coffee and baked oatmeal with camel milk, honey, walnuts and raisins.

> *Dear Henry,*
> *Greetings in our Lord's Name!*
> *We've been busy with births, ya, and the garden mostly. I don't know how to say this, it isn't easy, I don't think I'll get this right, but, see, um...your letter. I found parts of it upsetting. I don't know if I could be part of what sounded to me like judging others. I think perhaps we can agree to disagree with both ways: those that see the gut things about being in a conservative church, and those that are open more to the spirit of finding our way in the world we live in today. I don't think it has to be one way or the other so very exclusively, and then you cut off those you don't agree with and end it there. I don't think I could do that. It seems too legalistic. To give up what I believe so that I can be married and be submissive, it wouldn't be honest. I hope you can understand. I've prayed long and hard about this. I can only be honest, I think. Maybe Gott can find a way for us, but to disagree upon so much and we aren't even married yet, and...well, I can't see it. I hate to say it, but chust maybe you are meant to*

marry a Canadian Amische frau who more closely follows your way of thinking. Maybe our getting to know each other was meant to clarify your feelings and point you in the right direction. Maybe you would not see that otherwise. I am afraid I would not be a very agreeable companion. I must be chust too opinionated for my own gut. Please keep us in your prayers.

Hugs to Rose.
Veronica

She wasn't ready to actually mail it, though, not by a long shot. It would have to wait a few more days before she could be sure it was what she really wanted to say. After breakfast Veronica put on her faded gray work apron and *ditchly* not wanting to wear her good starched white *kapp* into the barn and went there to start the chores, mucking the stalls, feeding the animals, sweeping the forebay, filling the water troughs. The chicken coop was next on her list. The geese spied her but could tell she wasn't heading to the yard they'd staked out for the day, so there would be no fat, juicy slugs today. They could read that walk and it wasn't what they were looking at now. They went back to sniffing out bugs and grubs.

After the barn, the chicken coop was easy. Collecting the eggs, filling the feeders, checking their water, and letting the flock out for the day. There were only eight of them at present, though at least one broody hen could promise ten new chicks any day now. The sheep would keep for a couple of more hours and then she'd move them. There was plenty of fresh grass for them on the other side of the old farmhouse. They wouldn't go hungry.

Just then Veronica heard the sound of the little mail truck. She turned and confirmed, yes it was the mail. Dusting her hands off on her old apron she headed to the mailbox. She waved at the mailman as he drove off. Her palms were sweating.

Taking out the few letters there she closed the little mailbox door with a bang and stood looking at the envelopes one at a time. A bank statement, an invitation to an open house for a new pet spa in the area, Joann Fabrics coupons and there it was: a letter from Henry. Her heart skipped a beat, and not in a good way this time. She held her breath. The last letter was so upsetting. It took over two weeks *chust* to try to understand all it implied. She still didn't understand his reasoning as he laid it all out in that letter. *This one couldn't be much better could it?* she wondered. *Well, there goes today,* she thought to herself. *Bummer. Maybe I could accidentally leave it on the wood stove so I don't have to read it at all and go through all of that anguish and torment again...or I could buy a ticket and go volunteer in Siberia or somewhere where I could make myself useful. I am* chust *wasting time here with this...these...utterly exhausting mind games....*

After a bath and hair wash in the *kesselhaus* and hoping for a therapeutic change of scenery, Veronica decided to go see Pennelope. No-nonsense Pennelope. She wouldn't let Veronica mope in self-pity for long. No way. Not one to keep her opinions to herself she could be blunt. And she just might have some wisdom on the whole puzzle.

Her horse *redded* up, she backed the buggy out of the drive and onto the shoulder of the road. "I am *chust* glad I don't live in Ohio," she said under her breath. The fact was that the shoulders on most of the rural roads there weren't wide enough for a bicycle, much less a buggy. There are accidents there sometimes weekly. Last year there were eighty-four crashes involving buggies in the state. There have been 670 buggy crashes in Ohio since 2019 according to one report. Fannie at the general store had even told her they now have an Amish cemetery just for the victims of road accidents in Ohio. *So why can't the government put some money into widening the roads? The monster diesel semis barrel through at over fifty miles an hour most of the time on average on the narrow country lanes on their way across the state. Are there no other highways for them?* she wondered. *This* chust *goes on year after year. I don't get it,* she thought to herself as she clucked to the horse to pick up speed a bit.

She still hadn't read the latest letter. It was in her purse. Pennelope had seen the first letter. She'd promised Veronica that it would be on the top of her prayer list but couldn't offer any other insight at the time. She'd put her own unsent letter in her purse also, in case Pennelope wanted to see that one, too.

Veronica directed the horse up to the hitching post in the yard by a centuries-old oak tree where her horse commenced munching the lush grass and hoovering up the sweet acorns there. She knew Pennelope was home by the little buggy lined up by the others near the barn. It was the only one with plastic daisies wired onto the front window frame on the driver's side in the whole district, probably the whole state. *Maybe even the country,* Veronica wondered. Pennelope explained that it was getting harder and harder each year trying to find her own buggy amidst the sea of buggies off in a field after Sunday church or barn raisings, or school auctions. Veronica made a mental note to get some plastic flowers for her buggy. It was a brilliant idea. Maybe blue or purple ones.

Pennelope met Veronica at the door. "I hear tell by the grapevine you've been to another birth! How was it?" she was anxious to know.

"Ruth didn't even tell her when to start pushing," Veronica began while she was still removing her shoes and untying her travelling bonnet. "She said our bodies know what to do, *chust* like elephants and rhinoceroses! I'm learning so much I didn't know," Veronica told her as she peeled off her shawl and black bonnet and hung them in the mud room on a peg. Just then she heard a little squeak coming from the bedroom. Veronica followed Pennelope as she ran to the bed. Laying there was the most angelic baby Veronica had ever seen. Poppy was smiling, satisfied that her little fake cry had elicited the correct response from the grownups nearby. She began kicking and waving her arms while she cooed her delight that there were even two of them this time. A whole audience.

"Well, don't you ever get mad?" Pennelope asked the infant in her high-pitched *motherese* voice as she changed her diaper.

Veronica asked, "But if she's hungry or wet doesn't she cry?"

"Hardly. She knows we'll *kumm*," Pennelope explained. "She's gotta be the most trusting soul on earth. Here, you take her, she's got a clean diaper now and she'll be ready to eat soon." Pennelope dropped the diaper in a pail sitting by the nightstand.

Veronica hesitated a moment and then asked finally, "Did they get a final diagnosis on Poppy? The genetics people?"

"Oh, ya," Pennelope confirmed. "It is Downs. But, ya know, it doesn't matter what they call it. We're *chust* happy she's here and she quite healthy, but it's like we have our very own little angel straight from heaven. She's not like any other *bobbel* I've ever cared for. She is so very precious, so undemanding. Ya, she is a mystery. We don't know if she'll have health problems from it in the future. We don't know how much she'll be able to learn, or if she can even go to school. We can only really live one day at a time, ya know? By faith. We don't have a choice, really. These ones don't *kumm* with a road map or handling instructions."

Veronica slowly nodded. It was definitely uncharted territory. But Poppy was most assuredly a blessing.

"You'll stay for lunch?" she asked. Veronica followed her back to the kitchen with the baby on her hip while Pennelope washed her hands at the sink.

"If it isn't too much fuss," Veronica answered.

"None at all. And I want to hear all about that fiancé."

"Well," Veronica hesitated. "Well, he…um…might not be that anymore…."

"Oh dear! What's happened?" Pennelope quickly turned around to face Veronica, her wet hands dripping soap bubbles onto the floor.

"I'll fill you in," Veronica assured her, placing Henry's letter on the corner of the table. Diatribe would be more like it; his bitter attack against anything reeking of progress in the Church.

As Pennelope read the latest missive, Veronica bounced Poppy on her knees with the age-old game, singing the words, "This is how the gentlemen rides, clumpity, clumpity, clumpity…clump" bouncing her slowly, rather stately at first, and then "and this is how the lady rides, clackety, clackity, clackity…clack," while still bouncing the baby but a tad faster, and then the wild ride: "and this is how the baby rides," going even faster, "clippity-clop, clippity-clop, clippity," until baby falls into the folds of Veronica's dress between her knees which elicits all sorts of laughs every time.

"I'll *chust* take Poppy to her *mamm* first to nurse. It's her lunch time," Pennelope explained as she carried her precious cargo down the hall and into the main house. Veronica could hear the baby giggling as she disappeared into the other kitchen. Pennelope quickly returned and sat down at the table with the letter.

Veronica looked over at Pennelope who was still reading

the letter while shaking her head over what she was taking in. When she finally laid it down on the tablecloth, she just looked at Veronica with sadness written all over her face. She didn't know what to say. So, she didn't say anything at all.

Life is a journey, not a destination. Happiness is found along the road, not at the end of it.
- Amish saying

CHAPTER 15

Plum Ferhoodled

Veronica thought she was managing well enough. She was kept very busy canning the first crop of tomatoes and cucumbers. She tried to faithfully write in her journal every night. She got out of the house at least two times each week to help this or that one and kept up with her mending and garden in between times. The two quilted pillows for the upcoming wedding were finished and wrapped, ready to bring to the shower that was quickly coming up in another week.

The one thing on her to-do list that still needed doing was the Christmas cards she wanted to send, and the gifts she wanted to make. She'd managed to avoid buying gifts all these years and was hoping to continue that tradition, creating meaningful presents instead. Then she had a thought. *I could get everyone on my list a new harmonica from that* Amische *guy, Andy Weaver in Farmington, Ohio. I could send them out with peanut brittle. That would still be a homemade present? Sort of? And really fun.*

Then she remembered. *Where is that ad for the harmonicas?*

I saved it, I'm sure. She went to her bookshelf and found the Amish periodicals that she subscribed to.

"Here it is," she said aloud as she thumbed through them looking for the ad. She found it between North American Lantern Fuel in Kentucky and The Most Powerful Antioxidant Isotonic OPC-3, from Ronks, Pennsylvania. Finding the one she was looking for she read aloud to herself, "Enjoy harmonica tunes? Call the Harmonica Hotline! 1-234-900-5096 extensions 1 - 9. America's Harmonica Warehouse, Sugarcreek, Ohio. Orders; 330-231-2418." *Next time I go to the phone box then, she told herself.*

She was humming as she fixed her supper after a long afternoon of canning. That is, she was humming until she remembered the letter from Henry from the day before that had been conveniently forgotten and left in the bottom of her purse.

"Shuuuu-gar!" she growled. "I knew I'd forgotten something. I was hoping it was a *gut* surprise, and not that, though." She finished fixing the salad she'd been making for her supper and sat down at the table to eat it. *I'll read it after this,* she thought to herself. *I'm only going to get indigestion thinking about it.* She sat there for a minute after giving thanks. *Darn it,* she groused as she popped up to get the cursed letter from her purse hanging behind her bedroom door. Seated back at the table she opened the envelope.

> *Dearest Veronica,*
> *Greetings in our dear Lord's Name!*
> *I learned in school that a letter must begin with an introduction, then the body of the letter and after that a conclusion, chust like any gut story, but I apologize ahead of time because I don't think I can write that way today. I am wondering why I still have not heard from you. Are you sick? Has something happened*

there? I've been praying day and night that you are okay, but I still don't know what I can do, short of getting on the next bus and finding out for myself how you are. I'm beside myself with worry now. I chust can't not think about what has happened.

Have you somehow changed your mind? I can't imagine what might have precipitated that. I left you so encouraged, praising Gott for the miracle that led us together. And of course, Rosie is still asking after you. I thought for sure she would forget you if she wasn't seeing you every day, but that is far from the case.

So, I spend many nights wracking my brains, wondering what might have gone wrong. Edith thinks you might be having second thoughts about an instant family, meaning with kinner. That could be really hard for some, getting children that you want to love but aren't your own really. Then when others kumm along, can you really be impartial? She says you might be needing to start fresh, with a whole new family after all you've been through. I can understand that. Really, I can. That might be a real big milestone for some. I would hate to think that, but I would understand.

Or is it the letter I wrote after the visit? I am guessing I might have kumm on a little too strong, kind of heavy on praising our strict observance here in Canada and perhaps you took offence at my ideas judging the more progressive Amische in the U.S. Milo thinks that is what might have happened.

He also pointed out that perhaps I assumed wrongly that we would live in Canada and leave all your family and friede behind. I guess I should have asked some of these questions and not assumed everything. So, I came across unfeeling, too, chust thinking about how I feel about things, certainly not considering your feelings.

Then maybe you have met someone else. I didn't ask you if you had any other budding friendships in the works. You being such a sweet frau and all, perhaps you have been writing to others, beside me. It would be pretty darn brot of me to think I have been the first and only bruder you've ever written to. Granted, I am not exactly handhawwe or clever or young.

I can only guess. I've searched my heart over and over again wondering. I really need to know if there is something I said. Can it be fixed? I know this probably doesn't make any sense. It's ferhoodled for certain. I know I can't chust end our friendship like this, however. I am thinking perhaps we can talk through what you're thinking. I am deeply sorry if I offended you in any way. I am willing to go to the moon and back for you. Yes, it is making me plum ferhoodled, too. Well, maybe a lot ferhoodled.

This is the phone number of our gut English neighbors. You can leave a message there. We try to check it once a day or every other day. I don't know if you have an arrangement like that but please do leave a message if you can. 320-298-3679

I care very much for you. Please get in touch. Without knowing I can only imagine the very worst things down there, accidents and such.

Yours sincerely,
Henry

Well, that's interesting, she thought to herself as she carefully placed this latest letter on the tablecloth. *He knows how I feel now. Desperate. Unglued. Time to go see Aunt Wanda again I'm thinking. Maybe after chores in the morning. Desperate times call for desperate measures. Maybe I should* chust *go up there and see for myself. No,* she told herself. *That is plain over-the-top nuts. I'm not that far gone, yet. Hm. I think I am losing it. But maybe I should mail that letter I wrote after all. I still have it. It didn't get mailed. Maybe that would help sort out this* huddlich.

As she chewed her salad, she gazed over the two dozen

jars sitting on towels on all the flat surfaces in the kitchen, spaced just far enough apart to let them cool off after coming out of the canning kettle. She chuckled remembering the evening when she was about twelve when they brought *Dat* down to the root cellar to show him all the rows and rows of jars there, glistening with their rainbow of colors, so beautiful. Pink applesauce, green pickles, yellow mustard beans, white pears, red tomatoes and olive-green bread and butter pickles. He'd looked over them a bit and then laughing told *Mamm* that maybe he should *chust* buy a bunch of colored sand to fill her jars with and save her all that work.

Mamm *did this and taught us girls,* chust *like her* mamm *taught her, and going all the way back whole generations, like* Amische *and* Englischer *farm fraus have been doing for years and years. And we'll teach our girls the same things. If I have any* meedel *that is. I don't know. The possibility of that ever happening seems more and more remote I reckon. And I can't imagine the rest of my life without Rose in it. Who will teach her then, if I don't?* Ach! *What a mess I've made. It's absolutely* baremlich.

She finished her supper to the sounds of the canned vegetables pinging as the jar lids cooled, creating a vacuum in each. The food within would last all year this way, ensuring that no botulism or mold could form inside the jars. It brought back memories of when *Mamm* canned everything, and they'd fall asleep every night listening to the pinging coming from the kitchen down below.

Kneeling by her bed that night she began by asking for an extra dose of kindness. She knew she was sorely lacking in that department. It was not getting any easier to fend off Clara, her self-appointed matchmaker, and she felt increasingly uncharitable toward the woman. Clara really was looking out for Veronica and seemed genuinely serious about her happiness. Just the other day they bumped into each other at the health food store. Veronica tried her best to be civil, not cut her off or make a beeline to the other side of the store leaving Clara in the dust. Veronica wasn't in a hurry, so there was no need to rush off. She breathed a quick prayer, asking to be given just a little sympathetic understanding. Maybe just try harder to be accepting and generous toward her. Who knew what battles Clara might be fighting in her own life? At home? With her husband or kids? Money problems? There were a thousand things about her that Veronica would never know. Veronica should be the last person on earth to judge anyone. She had enough faults to sink a ship. And then some. She knew that. She didn't need reminding.

The other day when they'd met at the health food store Veronica had put on her best smile despite the aversion in her heart. *Beheef dich!* she admonished herself. *Behave now, you heathen,* she told herself. *You're such a hypocrite. No better than a pagan. Worse even. Thinking you're better because Clara can be so...so...unpleasant. And stubborn. A one-track mind. Not everyone has to get married....*

"Veronica, I haven't seen you in ages. I thought you might show up at the last quilting bee at Temperence's *haus*. Maybe you were off with the midwife, or maybe you were entertaining that beau. Did he visit again?"

"Well, if you must know, no, he hasn't visited. I'm not sure we're serious yet. Still getting to know each other 'from afar,' you'd say," Veronica said, hoping it would give her some time, putting Clara off for a spell.

"Oh, dear. I thought you would be betrothed by now. I wondered when I didn't hear the *banns* announced at church a while back, though I missed this last Sunday as I was visiting my *schwesters* in South Dakota for two weeks. My, was that ever interesting. They do so much different over there, bowl bonnets and all. Different capes, too. And the land is so flat, and dusty and you're in the middle of nowhere there. I can't begin to tell you. And they took us to see Mount Rushmore where they have those giant carved presidents' heads, though there was a protest or demonstration or something going on about the Native Americans blaming everyone else for desecrating their sacred mountains by carving them up without even asking permission first, which they wouldn't have given, mind you."

Veronica nodded in agreement before Clara cut in again. "Oh, and have I got a story for you!" Clara prattled on, even more energized by the fact that she alone could bring back the latest gossip from outside the district. She raced on with her news, hardly taking a breath.

"They've got *Amische* there migrating from the east here and other places, giving up on farming in the U.S., with milk laws getting tighter and the price of farmland. Anyway, they had lunch after church the Sunday I was there and there were all these families I'd never met, of course. And I was introduced to two *bruders. Ztzvilling.* They even look identical. And get this, Veronica." Clara laid her hand on Veronica's arm for emphasis, "Neither one is married! Well now, doesn't that take the cake then? I'm thinking you should go out there with me. We can go soon. Maybe you are supposed to meet them. I mean, it could be fate that I even went at all, ya know, and with things sounding like they're cooling off here in that department, who knows? They're both forty-two—of course I asked —and rather *gut* looking if you ask me," Clara added, dipping her head slightly and batting her eye lashes, while hoping for a positive response if not a thank you from her friend.

I don't believe this, Veronica thought to herself. *This is the giddy limit. Has the woman got no pride at all? So, I'm to marry both of 'em or what?* That thought made her laugh in spite of herself. "Clara, um, that's super interesting. Wow. I don't know, though," she said, stifling her laugh.

"There are a lot of fish out there in the sea," Clara said, nodding knowingly. "And you gotta get out there and *chust* find the right one, girl."

"I guess I am thinking I should *chust* pray...and trust, ya know," Veronica ventured a bit lamely, she thought afterwards.

"No, you can't test the Lord. You have to work, too; He can only give you the opportunity," Clara instructed.

Veronica raced to think of a way to end this debacle. "Well, that's mighty *gut* of you but I'll need to think on this, if that's okay. I've got a bunch of errands today so I best get on."

"Oh, I didn't tell *ya* what their parents named them. Ezekiel and Zacharia! Zeke and Zach. That's hysterical, *eh?* But then," Clara continued, "to my way of thinking, those two won't be single for very long, *ya* know. They're gonna be snatched up right fast, too."

"Maybe they're happy being *baetscher* farmers. Some choose that," Veronica tried to add, but Clara would have none of it.

"They *chust* haven't found the right ones yet. No one is meant to be a bachelor. You'd be perfect," Clara insisted. It was hopeless. Veronica knew she couldn't win this one, so she switched tactics. She wracked her brain for something that might derail Clara's one way train wreck.

Then it came to her. "Ya know, Clara, I was *chust* reading *The Diary of the Old Order Churches*. Do you get that one? I really like it. They listed all the twins born this year so far. It's quite entertaining. They had a whole bunch named

Mary and Martha. Then there was Aaron and Adam, and even Samuel and Steven...."

"Yes, I saw that," Clara cut in. Before she could take another breath Veronica ended the encounter.

"Well, *so* nice seeing you, Clara. Please keep me posted, okay?" she added charitably as she swung her shopping cart away and sped down the aisle to the checkout line.

That seemed to placate Clara for the moment.

"You stay well, now," Veronica turned back and called over her shoulder.

"You too," Clara responded, though it looked like she was thinking up more things to say.

Beat the high living costs: diet to prevent food shortage, take long walks to save gasoline. Your doctor will think this is good for your health, therefore you can also beat him out of the high cost of being sick! - Amish food for thought

CHAPTER 16

A Horse Named Rapunzel

She'd spent the day before with Eli and Hazel, putting their little *dawdi haus* to rights for the elderly couple. It was obvious that they were becoming less and less able to care for themselves. Veronica wondered if anyone, perhaps the ministers or their wives, had noticed and was thinking about how to support the couple better. They didn't have children who would otherwise take on their care. In this case it fell on the rest of the community. Veronica watched the slow decline week by week as she visited them. It was unheard of in the Plain communities to place the elderly in nursing homes like many English people do.

The place needed a good scrub, as in the floors, the walls and the windows. Even the ceilings were dripping with cobwebs. The cupboards and all the pots and dishes and mugs and glasses needed it too. There was plenty of mending if you looked closely enough at the elbows in the jackets and sweaters not to mention socks. The old folks had given up the chickens and the garden years earlier.

Eli still cared for their old buggy horse, though, who faithfully drove them to church or the occasional invite from a neighbor for dinner. She had been a former standardbred racehorse, known for their gentle temperament and used most commonly for pulling buggies. Eli purchased the beauty almost ten years ago at an auction. "Dirt cheap," he was quick to tell you if you asked. The buggy was another matter. A new one in Pennsylvania could set you back a full $9,000. The horse was almost never under $3,000 or $4,000. Eli talked the seller down to $1,500 for the horse. The seller must have taken pity on the elderly man to agree to that price. The buggy was decades old, having been inherited from a cousin.

Now her name was another story. She'd been dubbed Debutante in her former professional life of racing. But Eli couldn't be done with that name soon enough. Her name popped into his mind on the first day he rode her around the paddock. She had an unusually long thick black mane. It was long enough to braid and tie ribbons in for the races of her earlier life. Rapunzel stuck, even after Hazel repeatedly protested his choice.

"That poor old thing," she lamented.

"She won't know the difference," he reasoned. "And she ain't old. She could still live till fifty!"

"Well, I hope she ignores you then," his wife said in a huff.

"She's gotta listen," he explained. "I'm the one that's feedin' her," he chuckled. And he was feeding her exceptionally well, truth be told. He knew longevity in horses depended on superior nutrition, the single most important factor. He'd read everything he could about the breed and asked around at auctions when he'd attended. This horse would live to sixty if he had anything to do with it.

"Well, I know *chust* the girl for you, Veronica. This is definitely Divine Providence. I don't believe it," Ruth said shaking her head. "See, Sarabeth helped out in our district after that awful train accident almost two years ago now. The widow—Faith--kept her farm, she wasn't in the buggy that day. Her new baby either. She called her Patience. But it was a pretty big loss: her *halsband* and two little ones. So, Phoebe Schwartz, who is a nurse in their district—she's *Amische*—was helping out with the doctor involved, and well, in the end Sarabeth came from Ohio as a mother's helper. It really worked both ways. Sarabeth was impossibly unhappy and rebellious, and the family were at their wits end trying to find the right way with her. The teen years *chust* hit some harder than others. In her case they were turbulent years. Pretty bad from what I hear. Well, she came, and it worked out really well. Faith, the *mamm,* has since married and is expecting in a few months. She only has the other *bobbel,* and her *mamm* and *dat* are nearby, so Sarabeth could help here with Eli and Hazel until Faith needs her back. Sarabeth *chust* needed to be needed, and the job offered *chust* enough independence for her to blossom. I'll see what I can do, if she really can *kumm*. I can stop by her place tomorrow."

"That really would be amazing. Thank you so much. They really need another pair of capable hands I think," Veronica said. "Tell me about this nurse, though. She's not really Amish, is she?"

"Yes, she is. I know it sounds *ferhoodled*. So, the bishops all got together--this goes back around four years ago now-- and had a ministers' meeting to address all of the problems with too many C-sections, which might have been avoided and doctors taking advantage of the Plain churches and charging so much because we don't have insurance and they know we pay in cash. A lot of doctors wouldn't let us care for the elderly at home or help in any way. They assume we're practically illiterate, stupid cows. The abuses were terrible. Sticking one kid in the hospital because they claimed the family wouldn't know if he developed an infection after a pig bite. And get this: he was deaf and what hospital in South Dakota even has sign language interpreters? It was rather cruel is what it was. It's *Amische* money that is keeping that doctor's little rural hospital afloat. So he needs to keep it full, his own little kingdom. The list goes on and on.

"Anyway, the bishops asked Phoebe if she'd be willing to get her nursing license at the technical college nearby. The LPN program is two years. The Hutterites and some of the Mennonites had the same idea and sent their girls and they all got their degrees."

"Did Phoebe have any clue why they asked her? That must have been quite a shock, like *kumming* from outer space!" Veronica said.

"I agree. I hear it was quite a slog to get through. None of the girls had more than their eighth-grade education before that. They did alright though. The bishops *chust* wanted girls that were mature enough to handle it. Passed all their exams. Phoebe has helped some families who want to care for a dying *doddy* or *grossmammi* at home at the end, the way it should be. They also learned pretty quick that when you send a *frau* in to have a baby, those doctors will think twice about doing a Cesarean section with a nurse along to check on things. She has since had *ztzvilling* of her own but gets out plenty. *Chust* brings the *kinner* with her or her *mamm* watches them. You know the girls wherever she goes are always happy to hold a baby—or two.

"I heard tell she has a clinic once a week in the evening where anyone can come to ask health questions. She can refer them to a specialist and even make appointments for them or tell them if they need to see a doctor at all. The local doctors here at least couldn't be happier, either. They have someone now who can make sure their patients take their meds or follow a diet at home."

Veronica thought about that. "Weren't they worried that the girls would go all *Englische?* Dabbling in all that science and all that? Not to mention all the male students?"

"I'm sure it was a consideration, but they did so well. None of them were really *youngie*. They'd all been baptized and joined church already before going to college. That was a concern, a big consideration," Ruth agreed. "I still think you should get in touch with Phoebe and shadow her for a while. I've got her card here. She had the business cards made up to pass out so folks wouldn't forget her phone number at the phone box where they could leave messages, and her address if they wanted to write."

The Amish phone box is a relatively recent addition to Amish communities and can be found dotting Amish settlements across the country. Some are coin operated while others employ a party line serving two or more subscribers. You can call and leave a message which is usually checked fairly regularly.

For those Amish that don't use cell phones or have their own work phone rigged up in the shop or barn, the phone box is *the* way to hire a taxi, call family out of state or summon emergency services. There are usually enough in any given community so there is always one within reasonable walking, biking, or 'scootering' distance.

If you have the local phone box on your land, it will often be located close to the road, perhaps at the end of your lane, where neighbors can access it without having to come too far onto the property.

Why the phone box? The thinking behind it is that if the phone is not located in the home, it won't interfere as much with family life. The small inconvenience of having to travel some distance to use the phone discourages unnecessary calls.

Dr. Donald Kraybill tells in his book, *The Riddle of Amish Culture* that phones were first tested in Amish homes, and failed, in the early twentieth century. As they were found to encourage gossip and idle chatter, in-home phones quickly joined the list of taboo technologies.

The world was a better place to live in when people tried to get to heaven instead of the moon.
- Amish saying

CHAPTER 17

The Holy Toast and Yummasetti

Veronica still hadn't been to see Aunt Wanda. The last time she'd planned it she was summoned, albeit whisked away by the very annoying little pager from Midwife Ruth and had to leave in five minutes when the van would arrive, so Wanda got put on a rain check. Again.

Today should be different. No babies due immediately or overdue, though Ruth insisted babies come when *they* are ready, and not on the dates doctors and midwives assign to them. Veronica figured today should be safe, though she checked that she had the pager in her purse anyway, just in case.

She had Henry's latest letter in her purse also, along with the response she wrote but still had not mailed. She was afraid he just might show up any day now to see for himself what was going on. In the last letter he wrote he worried about all sorts of dire scenarios. Yes, his imagination was intact and active. He feared she'd been in an accident or had changed her mind for any number of reasons. She imagined he would not be put off for long. He certainly would not passively chock it up to the, 'well, it was not meant to be' kind of attitude that many Amish were brought up to believe.

Wanda would know what to do, if anything could clear it up, if anyone could. Veronica had run out of ideas. *This is* chust *too much,* she told herself as the buggy bounced along on the macadam shoulder of the road. *I can't keep going like this, this roller coaster ride. It is exhausting. I am too old for all this drama. Leave it for the* youngie. But then her mind brought up the picture of Rosie swinging on the rope swing in the yard on the last day of their visit.

The visage brought stinging tears back before she could blink. *What will happen to her?* she asked herself. *She is* chust *so precious. Maybe I will have to give up. Now that's a new thought. My understanding of submission and my questions about progressive versus conservative churches. Is that what is being asked of me? Is it really? It is hard to grasp that* Gott *would require that. Give it all up. It isn't exactly like I am being called to be a martyr. Not at all.* Chust *give up my opinions on everything. In the end we really don't know what* Gott *wants or who He even is. All our daydreaming and reading and discussions and debates that we carry around with us our whole lives, maybe He* chust *wants us to give it all up and trust. Then in reality all we can do is live each day at a time. Maybe we'd be happier if we could do that. Life would be a whole lot less stressful and complicated, for sure. We wouldn't have to worry about any of it.* Chust *live one day at a time. And here I was thinking I was so smart, so forward-thinking, but maybe I am* chust *like a hamster on a wheel going nowhere and wearing myself out in a hurry. And the rest of the world keeps going without me, whether I understand it or not....*

But Wanda actually *was* the right person to untangle this endless ball of knots.

The yard was full of children running this way and that as Veronica pulled her buggy over to the hitching post by the kitchen door of the main farmhouse. They stopped playing and stood silently frozen watching as she stepped down from the buggy and tied up the horse. The next moment the lunch bell rang out by the front door calling the family to dinner. The children instantly came back to life and raced to the door. Only the older ones held back and let Veronica in first. Lining up at the sink to wash up, the littlest ones stepping up on the little stepstool there, one of them turned to Veronica.

"Wanna play Red Rover with us after dinner?" he shyly ventured.

"Well," she explained. "I came to see your *grossmammi,* but maybe after that." He dejectedly turned back to scrub his hands. Then perking up he again addressed her. "Are ya staying for dinner? We're having Yummasetti. My best thing," he stated enthusiastically.

"Well, yes, then. That sounds absolutely yummy," she replied while he giggled. Then he addressed his mother. "*Mamm,*" he called across the kitchen, "she's staying. Say, what's for dessert?"

"Time will tell," she answered as she came back to the kitchen and supervised the hand washing until all were at the table. Their father was sitting at the far end of the table reading the paper before they came in. The baby was tethered in his highchair, bib already in place, happily waving a wooden spoon in each chubby hand.

The child directly behind the chatty one washing his hands swat at his back and whispered, "We're having Rhubarb Butter Crunch for dessert. I helped make it," she informed him.

"Oh! Veronica. I didn't hear you *kumm* in. You'll stay for dinner? Please?" Rhoda asked.

Just then Aunt Wanda shuffled into the kitchen from the *dawdi haus* door in her slippers and took her place in the armchair opposite Rhoda, smiling and nodding to Veronica.

The kitchen was warm, so welcoming from the chill outside this day. The sky was overcast. It could be threatening to rain soon. The wood stove was giving off plenty of heat which felt good. There were several pots sitting on the stove top waiting to be served up for the noon meal.

The expansive table was covered with a checkered oil cloth. A mantle lamp hung above it in the center. It was dim in the dining room but not dark enough to light the lamp quite yet. A tall stack of plates sat at the end by Rhoda's place where she was already sitting next to the highchair. There were three hand turned wooden jars spaced out down the center of the table each holding an assortment of standing forks, knives and spoons. A basket at each end of the table held folded cotton napkins within easy reach. When all was quiet their *dat* announced, *"Patties down,"* the signal for all to fold their hands in their laps under the table and close their eyes for the silent blessing. No one moved until he cleared his throat, indicating that the prayer was over.

Then *Dat* said, "Amen" to which one of the little ones on the bench answered, "and to the holy toast!" The grownups looked at one another, clueless as to where that came from.

Dat tried to figure it out. "Where did you hear that?" he asked quite perplexed.

"Well," the little one answered completely serious. "At church the minister was talking all about the Holy Toast and we was hungry for sure and then we sang and then it was time for lunch and they had that *gut* cinnamon toast that day."

At that *Dat* let out a huge guffaw. Aunt Wanda, Rhoda and Veronica each put a hand over their mouths and laughed too. Finally, Rhoda was able to collect herself and explained as she got up to serve dinner, "I think the minister was talking about the Holy *Ghost* on Pentecost Sunday." The children tried to take that in, quickly distracted again by the plates coming down the table that their *mamm* had filled.

Dat helped the children butter their bread from his end of the long table and poured water for them. The table was again quiet as everyone ate. The children knew not to talk during dinner unless asked. The children knew they were to be seen and not heard, and it was strictly observed in this family. At dinnertime at least. Now supper was another story.

"This is the best Yummasetti I've ever had I do believe, Rhoda. What do you all put in it?" Veronica asked.

"All the usual, you know: hamburger, onions, potatoes, celery, noodles," she counted off the ingredients on her fingers. "Then the peas, tomato soup, cream of mushroom soup, then the breadcrumbs. I toasted them in butter first, you know," she explained. "I use up the bread crusts and heels they don't eat all week and use those. I don't waste it that way. Then I dump on the grated cheese on top about fifteen minutes before I take it out of the oven."

"Well, I don't know what you do, but it's a whole lot better than mine!" Veronica said before taking another bite. "I made it for the last barn raising. We pot-lucked that one. We had a really *gut* turnout, not *chust* the potluck."

"Which one was that?" *Dat* wanted to know.

By the time a man gets old enough to watch his step, he is too old to go anywhere.
- Amish saying

CHAPTER 18
Barn Raising

"I think it must've been a couple of years ago. Jonas Miller's sugar bush was by their barn. They'd been boiling syrup every evening. The hay bales must have caught first and spread. They lost harnesses, a cruiser, a fore cart and his horses. The way he tells it, it burned to the ground in two minutes. The loft had over 2,000 hay bales," Veronica said.

Then *Dat* put down his spoon. "I bet you remember the big fires near Milroy, Pennsylvania in March 1992."

"How could anyone forget that?" she answered. The grownups all nodded at that.

Veronica added, "In the Kishacoquillas Valley, about seventy miles northwest of Harrisburg, right?"

"*Ya*, that's the one," *Dat* said. "He burned down six barns and a one-room schoolhouse all in one night within two hours," *Dat* explained shaking his head. "He was that bishop's grandson, too. Darvin Ray Peachey was twenty-three then, at the time if I remember correctly. And his *dat* still serving time for his arson sprees. Can you believe it? I remember standing next to the fire chief from Milroy and him saying, 'There's gotta be something wrong with him. It's hard to believe anyone would do something like that.' Those fires killed one-hundred seventy-seven animals just on the eve of planting season."

"Ya think he calculated that?" Rhoda wanted to know.

"I guess," *Dat* answered. "Isaac Yoder lost a barn and thirty-three cows that night. Oh, and seven horses, besides. Moses Hostetler told me 'you've got bad people and you've got *gut* people. That's for sure.' They lost more than cattle, for certain."

"I remember there was a total of one-hundred thirty-nine cattle lost and thirty-eight horses," Rhoda added. "Many of us Amish had already been plowing fields to prepare for planting that month, but those fires cost the families their horse teams, plows, and seed. The fires also killed dairy cows whose milk is the only source of income for many of those farmers during the winter."

Dat continued. "Twenty-four fire companies from four counties fought the fires, and a concrete company was drafted to carry extra water in its cement trucks."

Then Wanda spoke up. "After dousing the blazes, firefighters traveled from house-to-house warning farmers to watch their barns. They hadn't caught him yet by then."

"Everyone turned out to help," Rhoda added. The others at the table nodded. "There were bulldozers and dump trucks to bury the livestock carcasses in mass graves, all these *Englishers* staying up all night to pitch in and help. My! They made really quick work of it. And then the other trucks showed up and they got most of the debris cleaned out down to the foundations before the *Amische* vans brought all the *bruder* to raise the barns. Local lumber yards —English ones—donated a lot of the wood. Can you believe that? We'd never seen the likes of it. Over three hundred volunteers."

Then Aunt Wanda added, "You'd be setting up breakfast out on the tables for the workers and the trucks were all lined up in the field. Then the buggies would start *kumming*. As far as you could see the buggies came from all different directions leading to the farm. It was a sight to see. Hundreds of 'em. Some were walking alongside on the road too. It was literally a sea of horses, black buggies and straw hats. Young and old." Aunt Wanda shook her head at the memories.

"We *chust* cooked day and night to keep 'em fed. I remember that one," Rhoda said. "They planned to build a barn a day. Don't you know, two different *Englische* bakeries in town kept us stocked with free cookies and Danish and donuts the whole time too? They never let up. Amazing."

Aunt Wanda added, "They finally charged him with setting those fires that burned over one-million dollars' worth of barns and livestock. They brought in the federal authorities to help too," she said while nodding.

"But the story doesn't end there," *Dat* continued. "Oh no. That's when the donations came flooding in. And not *chust* from the U.S. but from abroad, too. More than 40,000 people from every single state and some foreign countries read about it and sent donations to repair the damage. Hang on here a minute," he said as he tossed his napkin on the table.

"Back then I kept a lot of the news clippings on this. Let me see if I can find that one," he said as he got up and walked across the creaky kitchen floor barefoot to the great room and up to the bookshelf there. He found the album he was looking for right away. Seated back at the table he smoothed out the page when he found it and proceeded to read.

"'The arrest of Mr. Peachey, who is being held on $750,000 bail, was the latest shock to the secluded Amish community here, a town of fifteen hundred where life proceeds at a 19th-century pace without most modern inventions like automobiles, tractors, electricity or indoor plumbing. Crime is so rare here that members of the Christian sect consider it a test of faith,'" he read.

"So is that how they do it?" he chuckled before continuing. "While the Amish simply turned the other cheek to the arson, their neighbors did not and pursued the case. Companies and foundations wrote big checks, schoolchildren sent single dollar bills, Germans sent marks, Texans sent horses and cattle, and within two months of the fires the Amish farmers were back in business. The donations covered nearly all of the farmers' losses, and checks still trickle in, but the self-reliant Amish are now returning new donations with a note of thanks, saying they are overwhelmed by people's generosity.

"The criminal case broke when Mr. Peachey's former fiancée and her mother recently recanted testimony they had given to a Federal grand jury. The fiancée now admits that she was with Mr. Peachey when she said he had set six barns and a former schoolhouse on fire with a propane torch. The fiancée's mother now also admits that she had testified falsely about the activities of her daughter and Mr. Peachey on the night of the arson. Under a plea agreement, the Walkers cooperated in exchange for being given the opportunity to plead guilty only to perjuring themselves before a grand jury rather than face more serious charges related to the arson. Prosecutors have recommended prison terms of twelve to eighteen months.

"Federal prosecutors are also charging Mr. Peachey with numerous instances of perjury before the grand jury and are seeking a prison term of up to fifteen years and fines of up to $750,000. And if Mr. Peachey is convicted of all of the stated arson charges, he would also face a prison sentence of one-hundred-forty to two-hundred-eighty years and up to $525,000 in fines. Mr. Peachey has no criminal record, but his father, Abraham Peachey, is a convicted arsonist who served three months in prison in 1965 for burning down his employer's barn. Neither father nor son are practicing Amish, but the younger Mr. Peachey's grandfather, Daniel M. Peachey, is one of about forty Amish bishops, or senior ministers, in the valley. And one of Bishop Peachey's neighbors, Samuel Moses Yoder, was one of the arson victims. 'I can hardly express myself,' said Mr. Yoder, who says he is still reeling from the disaster, the outpouring of help and the arrest of Bishop Peachey's grandson. And while he would not go so far as to say that he was glad that someone had burned down his barn, he did say that the experience strengthened his faith. 'It gets you stronger,' he said. 'It makes you want to get out and help other people.' The 53-year-old dairy farmer, who wears a bushy beard and clothes in the Amish style, spoke during a pause in working his sixty-acre farm.'"

At the mention of his 'bushy beard and clothes in the Amish style' a general muffled tittering rose up from the bench against the wall at the long table.

Dat stared them down and with just that one look they became silent. He continued reading.

"'He recalled being awakened in the middle of the night by firemen and seeing his barn, forty cows, fifteen horses and five pigs—his entire livelihood--disappear in flames and smoke. 'It was pretty cruel for all that livestock,' he said.

"Mr. Yoder said he immediately suspected arson because the one-hundred-year-old barn contained no electrical wires or inflammable liquids. But he said he never once harbored an angry or bitter thought. As he watched the fire die out, he recalled, 'I was hoping whoever did it would convert himself.' Still, Mr. Yoder, who has been asked to testify at Mr. Peachey's trial, also believes that 'punishment has its place here.' The arrest of the bishop's grandson is the talk of the Whitehall General Store, an Amish store here that sells everything from milking equipment to jugs of locust honey and boots. Harvey L. Yoder, the store's owner and a distant cousin of Samuel Yoder, said people were not vengeful. "They would not have done anything if the police hadn't stepped in," the store owner said. "The Amish are strong believers in non-resistance if someone does them harm. That is our procedure, the proper way of living, we think."

Dat continued reading. "'Someone from Texas offered a horse and said he would deliver it himself,' said the head of the local bank handling relief efforts. Kishacoquillas Valley Bank set up a Big Valley Barn Fire Relief Fund to help the families, and Hayes said extra people had to answer the phones as calls came in with offers of aid. The phones were 'ringing off the hook,' he said. 'We had calls from Hawaii, California, all over the South and Midwest, Seattle and a lot from the Los Angeles area. Most of the calls promised support, some of it substantial,' Hayes said, but checks hadn't come in yet, so he had no idea of the amount of money contributed.

"The Mifflin County extension office is coordinating donations of items like building materials. The families don't have space to store donated building materials, so county officials asked contributors to hold onto those gifts until they are actually needed. Ivan Peachey, district coordinator for the Mennonite Disaster Service, said more than three hundred volunteers cleaned up the damage from the fires. "It's just remarkable how the people turned out," he said. Peachey estimated that materials for construction of one basic barn—with all volunteer labor—will run about

$50,000. That's the rough barn, not one thing of the equipment in the barn," he said. Peachey's wife, Ruth, said that they had received a call from people in Kansas wanting to know the number of cattle each family lost. The callers wanted to donate cattle according to the number lost. Another caller from Washington state offered to send seed to the farmers for their Spring planting." Everyone was quiet then. The children were licking a finger and silently gathering any last crumbs from their dessert dishes. Sulvilla, their second grader raised her hand then.

"It's not school, honey. You don't have to raise your hand here," her *mamm* said, chuckling. "What is it?"

Sulvilla blushed. "*Dat,*" she hesitated. "What is arson?"

It's a big job to build a sunny future on a shady past.
- Amish saying

CHAPTER 19

Playing On The Outhouse Roof

Dat excused the children with explicit instructions to do their afternoon chores. The older ones had their assigned duties and went directly to them. The youngest ones were charged with tagging along with an older brother or sister to learn alongside them. This system usually worked well until someone thought up a way to get out of the work altogether and employ their little shadow with the whole task. Then they could go up to the hay loft and shoot marbles or play cards, only needing to check on their little slave periodically.

On very rare occasions the younger one might suddenly wise up to the ruse and go hide too, forcing their task master to have to find them *plus* finish their assigned jobs. Today it was Suvilla's turn to follow her big sister Lena around. Lena wanted to play with the baby goats, so she set Suvilla up to change the water in all the rabbit hutches. There were twenty-four rabbits living in twelve cages. That would keep her busy a good long time. She gave her a bucket with a dipper and showed her how to unlatch a cage door, dump out the old water, fill the water dish with fresh water and then lock the door back up again.

Suvilla had other ideas, however. As soon as Lena was out of sight, Suvilla skipped down the aisle in the large hut where the rabbits lived and unhooked all the doors. She thought this might save time. She ran back to the bucket and ladled out the water and ran back to the first cage. The ladle was empty, much to her surprise. She tried again, this time watching the water in the ladle, being more careful not to let it spill over the edges on her way back to the cages.

While she stood there pondering this phenomenon, she looked up to see bunnies leaping from the doors of their cages and scooting in all directions in the shed. She knew she couldn't possibly catch them all. It was futile. Boy, was she gonna get it.

She tossed the ladle back into the bucket where it landed with a splash and headed out behind the barn. She peaked around the corner once she was outside and finding no one, headed for her favorite haunt. Climbing up the ladder there she stepped onto the outhouse roof and to her surprise another little fugitive was hiding up there already. They lay on their stomachs looking out over the top of the slanted tar-papered roof. No one could see them, but they could survey the entire barn yard from their hiding place.

They watched the pigs snuffling and rooting around for their slop. They looked pretty miffed that it wasn't already in their trough. Then they watched the donkeys heading in from the paddock. They knew this was about time to look for grain in their stalls. Guinea hens were pecking the dirt on the drive while sending up a din that would wake the dead, to no one in particular. Suvilla pointed out the geese to her companion. There was quite a flurry of excitement on the lawn where one of the bigger children was tossing grain toward them from a bucket.

Back in the kitchen Veronica hefted the chunky baby out of his highchair and took him to the sink to clean him up. She had him facing the sink while she secured him with her right arm, using her left hand to scoop up dish water and scrub his face, hands, arms, and neck. There was food everywhere. When he appeared clean enough, she offered to diaper him which Rhoda gratefully agreed to. This task turned into what essentially was a wrestling match. This one knew how to flip out of your grasp the second you went for a diaper pin. You'd have to rewrap him in the cloth diaper and try again, though more times than not he would outwit you, twisting this way and that while laughing uproariously.

Returning to the kitchen Rhoda told Veronica he could be put him down to graze on the floor. Of course, he found tiny crumbs on the floor that immediately went into his mouth. After five children, Rhoda ignored most things they put in their mouths. They would most likely build up their immunity by ingesting all sorts of germs, she figured. Then she smiled at the memory and shared it with Veronica.

"I saw him at a recent picnic on the grass where I'd parked him. He actually popped a caterpillar into his mouth. I jumped up from my seat and ran over to rescue it. When I got there his mouth was empty and he had only half a caterpillar in his little fist. That cured me, for sure. I stopped sterilizing his stuff after that. The only difference is when any of the children have been in the barn during the day, then they will definitely be needing a full bath before bedtime. There are no exceptions to that one," she concluded.

"I was a *youngie* when we heard about the 1992 fire*. It was all they talked about for months after," Veronica mused. "I'd never wish a fire on anyone, but it sure was exciting to help with the food and clean up and watching the cooks' *kinner* and then when the vans pulled in with *youngie bruder* from places I've never even heard of much less been. They came from all over the states around us. Each family here had to set up a guest room and squash as many into it in sleeping bags and all and put them up for the week or however long they could stay.

"We weren't supposed to fraternize—you know what I mean—but you sure wondered what they were thinking too. A few managed to meet up in the evenings, but my *mamm* wouldn't hear of it. That was fine because four of them were staying with us and after showers and supper we'd play board games and such for a bit, so it was okay.

"Amos was on one of those trips. I caught him looking at me every lunch time when we'd set out all the food right there in the yard so they could eat and then get back to work. We washed and rinsed and dried them, then reset the plates right at the tables outside to save time. We each brought the dishpans with soap and one with rinse water out to the picnic tables and ran it all through right there, ready for the next sitting. We kept snacks and *kaffi* at the tables between the meals. At first, I thought I was imagining it, but it became every day. I was real busy setting tables and resetting them, so I wasn't *chust* standing there scanning the place for him, but he managed to be close enough when the lunch bell rang so I kept seeing him. I think the third time I smiled back. And so did he. That was the first time I ever got butterflies. I'd imagine marrying

---

* This is a true story that appeared in numerous English and Amish newspapers that year, 1992.

this one or that one growing up, ya know what that's like around eighth grade? Even playing volleyball I'd pick out one and think, 'what would he be like?'"

"Another time we were caroling, and the sleigh came by our place and me and my older sister ran out of the house when we heard them *kumming*. We'd arranged to do it after supper one Sunday night. We were all bundled up and when we jumped up into the sleigh it was packed like sardines. Boys were literally sitting on the floor but we *chust* sat on each other's laps, between us girls of course. I got butterflies then. Some *buwe* was sitting on my boots. That was the closest I'd *kumm* to butterflies then.

"But Amos was different. Like a whole planet different. He managed to ask me for my address and was it okay to write to me. I was sixteen so I said yes, but that I'd have to ask my *mamm*. He wrote such sweet letters. I'd get butterflies again *chust* walking to the mailbox sometimes. I shared them with *Mamm*. You'd think it was her getting *liebesbreifs* she was so excited."

"The next time I saw him was when the Stutzman's goat barn burned down. The milkhouse along with all the hay and straw, bulk tank and milking machines all burned to the ground. The gasoline motor on the straw-hay chopper backfired, they figured, and sent sparks out which caught fire in the hay. The boys used their coats and had it out but then it flamed up again and was ablaze in a short time.

"He came with another trip about six months after that with a bunch from home to help again that time too. We weren't courting yet, but *Dat* said we could go walking after supper. That was my first date with anyone, though it wasn't really a date. We didn't even hold hands yet. That came later when we officially courted.

"At the time I thought I'd be all embarrassed to be seen with him but it *chust* was very natural. We were best friends right from the beginning. Eventually he came—this was three years later after we'd both joined church—on real visits. And then I thought he'd never pop the question, but he finally did. Funny how you are so afraid it will never happen, that time is *chust* going at a snail's pace and it will all pass you by when you're young. All the fretting and agonizing you do. As if you can change anything with all your worrying, while all the time you forget *Gott's* part in bringing you together and His plans for you." Rhoda and Aunt Wanda nodded sagely in agreement.

It is a good idea to keep your words soft and sweet. You never know when you may have to eat them.
- Amish saying

CHAPTER 20

Flat Squirrels

"Do you know how long I've been trying to see you?" Veronica asked the dear old lady as they walked over to her little *dawdi haus* apartment off the main farmhouse. Wanda nodded. Then she spoke.

"I read the letters you left me. It's complicated, eh?"

"That's an understatement. It's crackers. I'm sorry I ever agreed to this," Veronica said.

"Oh, don't say that. It's not hopeless," Wanda reasoned.

"Ya think? I don't know. I'm ready to throw in the towel. I think I've had enough."

"Did you send your last letter that you told me about to him?" Wanda wanted to know.

"No," Veronica said. "I *chust* don't have the courage anymore. I think he's probably too set in his ways."

"But he says he loves you. Do you believe that?" Wanda wondered.

"Sure, he can say it, but if we marry and fight over every little thing year after year that won't last long," Veronica answered while shaking her head. Then she continued.

"I'm not sleeping well at night. Everyone keeps asking

me if we've set a date; they all want to know where we'll live. What am I supposed to tell them? That I've changed my mind 'cause I don't want to be a submissive wife, pandering to his every whim and his *ferhoodled* theories about this and that?"

"Well, I don't think *Gott* has given up yet. I think my cousin in Missouri sent this to me for a reason. She didn't know about you and your struggles. I haven't mentioned it. It's funny, though. It made me think of you both right away. I didn't understand it at first, but I think if you look at it with the eyes of faith, you might *chust* get a glimpse of His workings. It actually blew me away. It might do for you too. I'm thinking you might also send it to him. Think about it. I can't think of any other way for you two." Then Wanda opened the envelope that she'd left on the little table in her bed-sitter. Veronica sat back in her chair, wondering what the letter could possibly contain.

Wanda explained as Veronica smoothed out the letter, "Lucy says no one can find out who wrote it or where it came from. Different ones are sending it in to be published in ladies' journals and all. I'll let you read it. I'm going to bring in the wash," she said as she shuffled back outside. "I won't be long."

Everyone longs to give themselves completely to someone—to have a deep soul relationship with another, to be loved thoroughly and exclusively. But God says, "No, not until you are satisfied and fulfilled and content with being loved by Me alone. I love you, my child, and until you discover that only in Me is your satisfaction to be found, you will not be capable of the perfect human relationship that I have planned for you. You will never be united with another until you are united with Me—exclusive of anyone or anything else, exclusive of any other desires or longings. I want you to stop planning, stop wishing, and allow Me to give you the most thrilling plan existing—one that you can't imagine. I want you to have the best. Please allow Me to bring it to you. Just keep experiencing that satisfaction knowing that I AM. Keep learning and listening to the things I tell you. You must wait.

Don't be anxious. Don't worry. Don't look around at the things others have gotten or that I've given to them. Don't look at the things you think you want. You just keep looking off and away up to Me, or you'll miss what I want to show you.

And then, when you're ready, I'll surprise you with a love far more wonderful than any would ever dream. You see, until you are ready and until the one I have for you is ready, I am working even this very minute to have both of you ready at the same time. Until you are both satisfied exclusively with Me and with the life I have prepared for you, you won't be able to experience the love that exemplifies your relationship with Me...and this is perfect love.

And dear one, I want you to have this most wonderful love, I want you to see in flesh a picture of your relationship with Me, and to enjoy concretely the everlasting union of beauty and perfection and love that I offer you with Myself.

Know that I love you utterly, I am God. Believe it and be satisfied.

— ANONYMOUS

Several minutes went by as Veronica stared at the letter. The only sound in the house was the clock on the wall ticking. Veronica didn't know what to think. It had rendered her speechless.

After several more minutes passed, she remembered what she'd read in her little devotional calendar just this morning on her dresser. It didn't make much sense at the time. Just a nice, encouraging saying, but nothing that could move mountains. Not like this. But she'd wondered about it just the same.

The battle in which you are engaged demands courage. Your goal is to love as God wants you to love, so as to be fearless. Perfect love alone casts out fear. Nothing else can do it. So you must learn to love perfectly!
- Catherine Doherty

Be decisive. Right or wrong, make a decision. The road of life is paved with flat squirrels who couldn't decide.
- unknown

CHAPTER 21

Macaroni and Cheese

Every time she tried to visit them something always came up. Last time it was a birth. Today Veronica planned on stopping in to see how Eli and Hazel were getting on with their new *maud,* Sarabeth. They were getting older and less and less able to care for themselves. They had never had children who could look after them in their old age.

As she turned into the long driveway, she saw Eli coming out of the barn. He heard her rig and waved her up to the hitching post.

"*Gut* to see ya," he practically yelled. *I bet he isn't wearing his hearing aids,* Veronica thought to herself.

"So nice to see you," she said as she climbed down and shook his hand. Before she had a chance to ask, he dove right in as if he had rehearsed his report.

"That *meedle* you found for us is a gem. A real gem. And can she cook too! That girl is one in a million. Hazel can't get over it either. She doesn't grump or complain about anything, *chust* works real hard and keeps it all rolling nicely.

Yes sir, we'll keep her. And we're mighty grateful for you finding her for us."

"Well, I can't tell you how happy I am to hear that, Eli," Veronica said.

"And she's funny, too. I caught her riding bareback out in the paddock the other morning. Never met one *chust* like her," he shook his head as he continued.

"Well, *kumm* in. Almost dinner time. I dunno. Maybe not quite time. Anyway, she won't tell me what she's fixing to eat. *Chust* says it's a surprise," Eli said, chuckling over his shoulder as he led the way to the kitchen.

Veronica was carrying in a pan of sourdough sticky buns. She'd remembered that Eli really liked them. When they got to the kitchen door he spun around and grabbed the pan.

"Here, I'll take those," he said as if he was afraid they'd disappear on him. "You take your *shors* off then," he said as he indicated the mat in the mud room.

Veronica laughed in spite of herself. He was in a better mood than the last time she'd seen him, when the house was in such disarray. She looked around as she walked further into the house. Taking off her shawl and travelling bonnet she hung them on a peg.

The house was tidy. The piles of plates and pots that filled the sink on her last visit were gone. There were no stacks of newspapers waiting to cascade onto the floor nor overflowing waste baskets. As she walked into the kitchen Sarabeth ran across the wood floor barefoot and enveloped Veronica in a huge hug. Veronica could see Eli over Sarabeth's shoulder as she was being warmly embraced. He was by the dry sink dipping his finger into the pan of sticky buns and quickly popping a fingerful of goo into his mouth.

"How are you? This is so nice. Can ya stay for dinner? I

hope so. I made Eli's favorite, mac and cheese," Sarabeth pleaded.

"Ya, of course. So this is working out ok?" Veronica asked looking deeply into Sarabeth's eyes.

"It's the best. Thank you! A thousand times! I love it here. I have my very own *doddy* and *grossmammi* to spoil all I want," she said.

Veronica was convinced. She had prayed long and hard that the arrangement would suit all parties. This was indeed good news, even better than she'd hoped. Sarabeth was genuinely happy, not the sullen, belligerent adolescent she'd been when she first came to help Faith after the accident.

Hazel was sitting at the table snapping green beans when Veronica came in.

"But you haven't told her the biggest news yet, Sara," Hazel prompted.

"Oh, yeah. I'm courtin'. Since last week! Can you believe it? I joined church before I left Faith's and met him at the first singing I went to here. Oh, you'll love Benuel," Sarabeth said as she stirred the pot on the stove.

"That is *gut* news. My! Whatever next? I bet your folks are so proud of you, too, eh?" Veronica asked.

"They'd about given up on me before Faith's place. I guess I was rather incorrigible," she laughed.

"I don't know if you know this, but sort of at the height of those years, my *mamm* told me your parents even consulted with that mental health clinic—Spring Haven--asking if there were any medications that might help you. They were at their wits end, if I remember correctly. They *chust* felt so badly that they couldn't find the right way with you, and you were so very unhappy. One social worker said you were irredeemable. Can you believe that? She said you were what's called a 'habitual delinquent,'" Veronica explained.

"No!" Sarabeth said, visibly shocked. "Really?"

"It's true. They heard she was fired shortly after that. I don't think she was very reliable with her diagnosis. Anyway, they tried everything back then."

"Yeah, I remember those psychology tests they did at that place," Sarabeth said.

"At one point they even told your parents you weren't hyperactive or autistic, which was a relief," Veronic added. "They said all they could find was that you were gifted."

"Huh? What is that?" Sarabeth wanted to know, frowning.

"They told your folks that you were an 'other thinker,' not like most kids but you were super intelligent. That if they could connect with you on some level, you might get sorted out, somehow. They weren't very helpful in the end. It didn't really make sense. Your parents blamed themselves, having only an eighth-grade education. They thought maybe you would do better with a tutor rather than attend school, but that also didn't pan out. Anyway, look at you now. I bet they are so very, very proud of you, too," Veronica said.

"*Gott* works in mysterious ways," a little voice from the table said. Hazel held up the bowl of beans for Sarabeth to take. "We couldn't be happier," Hazel added. "It's like she is our very own...the one we waited for all those years, and they never came. He knew we were waiting for Sara. He is so *gut*, eh?"

You can live without music, you can live without books, but show me the one who can live without cooks.
- Amish saying

CHAPTER 22
To Have and to Hold

Dear Kitty,

I haven't written in chust too long. Where does the time go? Well, a few things to report here. I revised the letter to Henry and sent it. Then I sent him the letter that Aunt Wanda gave me. That was so strange, her getting that in the mail and knowing it was meant chust for me, for us. Well, I'll tell you, he was relieved that I hadn't died. He wrote back. The letter from Wanda affected him, too. He wrote the most beautiful confession back. So there is hope for us. It is hard to believe. I was sure I would be calling it all off. I didn't think we were compatible in the end. Not at all, really.

Then that letter, like Gott was ready to speak directly to us, but maybe we were finally ready to hear Him? It's so humbling. It's like we think we know the Bible and the teachings of the Church, we grow up with them, we think we are living it each day, and being Amische being doubly observant and then reality hits you. We thought we knew it all, were so very smart. We know nothing of Him and the next world. It really is like looking through a veil. I feel like I got it all wrong. It's like I am a bobbel all over again, starting again, from scratch.

A whole deeper level, all my intellect and reasoning meaning absolutely nothing now. But now we both trust He will show us the way. Amazing. I don't know where this all comes from. A whole new chapter. Another chance, for sure.

Dear Veronica,
Greetings in our dear Lord's Name!
I wish I was there and could tell you how sorry I am for all of your hurt and what part I played in all of it. I for sure bungled this one. I had no idea. That's what pride does to you. I was so very full of myself and my ideas and had lost sight of the most important things. I could have lost you if Gott hadn't stepped in. I was so blind, eh? I would understand if you can't forgive me now. I brought it all upon myself. Arrogance. All of it. I really don't know how I can make it right now. I think that's why men need a help mate. They chust have to be humble enough to listen when the other sees something that you don't. The trick is not to both be deluded at the same time. Then the ship will really sink. Promise me you'll never be afraid to tell me what you are thinking, please. Even if you aren't sure you are right. You have my permission to kick me if I go off the rails again. See this is why Gott put us together, 'cause I am so thickheaded. I need someone who loves Gott and will listen to Him.

I thought marriage was mostly chust being happy together, agreeing together with each other, and my job was to lead in that. Well, I can see now I was driving the buggy right over a cliff. I could have lost you forever, I know that now. I really can't tell you how very sorry I am. I don't know if you have the courage to move on, for us to go forward. I pray you do. I am going to trust your instincts on this. Chust tell me what you think we should do next. I will be waiting for a letter back,

okay? I sincerely ask your forgiveness. I am sure this won't be the last time I ask that.
Please write soon.
Your bruder in Christ,
Henry
P.S. Rose is still asking everyone she sees, including her doll, where you are.

Veronica tucked the letter under her pillow. So many thoughts flooded in as she lay down and pulled the quilt up to her chin. Gratitude mostly. So, they really were two very much alike, needy souls. 'Sitting on the same bench' the ministers called it in church. 'Warts and all,' others described it. So Henry wasn't hopeless after all. She had started to wonder that in the preceding weeks. She'd always assumed she wouldn't be any easier to live with, with all her questions and fanciful ideas. If only they could avoid any more roadblocks like this in the future, though, but she realized no marriage is without those. They would have plenty of those ahead of them but *chust* maybe they were now slightly better prepared to face them. At least they were both in a more humble place now to start with. Marriage was such hard work. In reality the struggles never end. But then you had each other, "to have and to hold, in sickness and in health, till death do you part."

I suppose if we always knew what was ahead, we'd never get married at all, Veronica mused as she fell asleep.

Spanking a child to get him to behave is like driving your buggy by honking the horn.
- Amish proverb

CHAPTER 23
Fugitives

The next morning Veronica knew exactly what she had to do. First, she'd go see Aunt Wanda. She had to have her help with this new scheme. She was on a mission. Then, once she'd gotten her to agree to the whole thing she'd need to go to the next farm and get one of their boys to take care of the chores for a few days. She couldn't think of anything else that needed doing besides that. She could leave a note in the mailbox letting the postman know she'd be back in a week or about that so the mail wouldn't pile up.

And she'd have to check in with Ruth so she could get another midwife from the clinic to back her up for a few days should a baby decide to arrive in the meantime. *Well, not exactly in that order, I'm thinking* Veronica told herself.

The next item on her to-do list was to pack. She opened her suitcase on the bed and laid out everything she'd need. She'd pack light. No need to carry around a suitcase that weighed a ton. Clothes, toiletries and couple of books went into the suitcase. Kitty, too, her name for her journal. Zipping it up she grabbed her purse and went downstairs.

Food, she told herself. *Peanut butter and jelly sandwiches will last just fine without refrigeration. Dried fruit, nuts, some cans of juice,* she listed her other options. *Pretzels,* she mentally added to the list. Those all went into her carpet bag. *Some paper napkins and cookies. Apples. I have two somewhere around here. We won't starve. I can go get Wanda last and leave the horse and buggy with them. Write the mailman first,* she reminded herself.

Sitting down at the table Veronica ate her breakfast while penning a note to leave in the mailbox. Filling up her thermal to-go mug with coffee she grabbed the suitcase and swung the carpet bag strap over her shoulder. Then she threw her shawl over her arm and picking up her purse she headed out the door. Halfway to the barn she remembered her black travelling bonnet.

"Darn," she said under her breath. Leaving the suitcase there in the yard she hurried back to the house and grabbed the bonnet. She tied it on and continued on to the barn. Unloading it all into the back of the buggy, she hitched up her horse.

"I must be losing it this time, for certain," she addressed the horse. "But desperate times require desperate action. You get this, eh?" The horse actually nodded at the appropriate time in response. Well, it sure looked like that, anyway.

"Here goes nothing," she said to no one in particular. "Mailbox. Then the Ech's farm to get Enos to check things here while I'm gone. Okay. Then Ruth and only then Wanda's last," she mapped it all out in her mind.

Stopping by the mailbox at the end of the driveway, she pulled on the reins to stop the horse and hopped down from the bench seat to put the note in the mailbox. Putting up the red flag on the mailbox, she returned to the buggy.

It was only five minutes to the Ech's farm. Driving up to the hitching post she secured the horse and knocked at the kitchen door. It was plenty early but there was a light in the kitchen so she knew someone was up. She explained her request to Enos when his mother came to the door.

"*Ach,* for sure. He can do that. Have a *gut* trip," she said to Veronica. "Wanna *kumm* in for a *kaffi* first?" she asked.

"No, but *denki* so much, though. Bye." She waved as she turned toward her horse to untie the rope.

Okay, Ruth is next, she thought to herself. *I hope she can find a replacement for me while I'm gone.*

"You're what? Are you kidding me? And he doesn't know?" Ruth was horrified. Aghast.

"That's right. I decided last night," Veronica replied.

"But that's *ferhoodled...insch* even!" Ruth said, appalled. "What are you thinking?"

"That desperate times call for desperate measures. I can't get into everything now, but I think it's the right time. Trust me, Ruth," Veronica begged.

"Trust you when you are off your rocker? No, I don't believe this," Ruth argued. Then Ruth continued.

"Besides, you really think all that conservative stuff will magically go away? Or that you can live under that tyranny? *Really?* Please be reasonable, Veronica," Ruth begged.

"I will let you know all the gruesome details when I get back, I promise. *Chust* pray for me now, will ya? *Please?*" Veronica entreated her friend who only wagged her head in desperation.

"I can't imagine...." was all Ruth could reply. Veronica went back outside to untie the horse. As she drove down the driveway, she looked back to see Ruth standing in the open doorway covering her mouth with one hand, the other one lamely waving goodbye.

Well, that's sort of what I expected, Veronica told herself. *Ruth is so practical. Never been very daring. Never even went down to Pinecrest, Florida. I'd really like to go down there with her. I wonder if our single ladies' group would do that this summer? A vacation. But I might be married by then. Who knows?* thus went the conversation as Veronica drove the buggy, this time to Aunt Wanda's. It was a longer drive. Maybe thirty-five minutes or so. Plenty of time to ponder the pros and cons of this quest.

I wonder what he'll say when he opens the door. Or if he is off doing chores comes home and finds us at the table waiting for him... I'm sure he's gotten my letter by now. And I got his. So we are on the same page now, so to speak. Nothing stopping this escapade now. I hope, Veronica told herself, now doubting the whole premise of visiting him unannounced for the first time.

No, I think it'll be gut. *Something we will tell the grandchildren years from now,* she thought, smiling. *I wonder how many there will be? Grandchildren. Now stop this right now, youse,* she admonished herself.

She pulled up to Aunt Wanda's farm where she'd lived in the *dawdi haus* going on ten years now. She saw the curtains parting and then pulled shut once again. Wanda opened the door and waited for Veronica to come in.

"So *gut* to see you! *Kaffi?*" her aunt asked as she ushered her in.

"Oh yes, *denki*. I need to talk with you," Veronica prefaced her rehearsed speech. It had to be convincing. She'd come this far. Wanda was the only missing piece in the puzzle. She hung up her things on a peg and sat at the kitchen table.

"Well, then tell me about it," Wanda said as she puttered about the tiny kitchen putting on coffee for her guest.

"Well, I had this brainstorm last night. I decided that after all those letters and making up and everything, that I want to go up to Canada and surprise him. We need to talk and make plans, and we could write letters until the cows *kumm* home, but I need to be sure. I need to hear it from him. Is that so nuts?" Veronica asked.

"Oh. Well," Aunt Wanda was taken aback. "I guess that makes sense," she said, blinking.

"But I need you to go with me," Veronica explained. "I can't go all that way alone. It wouldn't be right," she added.

Aunt Wanda plunked the coffee percolator down hard on the stove top. "Oh my!" was all she could answer.

"See, you'd be perfect. We'll have all that time to visit on the way. It will be fun," Veronica explained further. "The Greyhound bus leaves here at ten tonight. You've got plenty of time to pack and we'll call a taxi and leave the horse and buggy here with your family. I've taken care of everything else already."

"You've got someone to look after your chickens and sheep?" Wanda wanted to know.

Veronica nodded her head. "Yup, they're all covered."

"What about your midwife? What if she needs you?" Wanda inquired.

"All taken care of," she stated. "And I've got food all packed for the trip, though we can get hot *kaffi* or cocoa when the bus stops along the way."

"What will I bring?" an increasingly, very flustered Wanda wanted to know.

"*Kumm,* I'll help ya," Veronica said.

"Well, I guess at my age I'm up for a little adventure," she said, and then under her breath, "I must have a loose screw somewhere, I reckon, to talk me into this…this…foolishness."

They packed Aunt Wanda's suitcase then. When it was done, Veronica reviewed the list they'd made so they wouldn't forget anything.

"Toothbrush and denture paste," Veronica read.

"Yes," Aunt Wanda replied in the affirmative.

"Pills," Veronica asked as she crossed that off the list.

"Yes, check."

"Slippers and nightie."

"Yes."

"Unmentionables?" Veronica asked. That was what Aunt Wanda's generation called underthings, underwear and such. "We don't talk about such things in polite company," she had been told.

"Yes."

"Bathrobe?"

"Check."

"Purse and ID?"

"Yup. Got that," she replied.

"I can't think of anything else, can you?" Veronica asked.

"We *chust* have to call the van lady to pick us up to drive to the bus," Aunt Wanda said.

"Gosh! I would've forgotten that. Thanks. Yes. I'll go out to the phone box. Then we'll go next door to the kitchen and tell them," Veronica said.

Everything was taken care of by 3:00 p.m. when Aunt Wanda and Veronica made their way to the big house where Rhoda's family lived with their five children (plus one on the way.)

Rhoda was at the stove beginning supper. Their toddler was in his highchair banging a plastic set of measuring spoons on the tray while watching the Cheerios put there for his afternoon snack skittering around every time he banged the spoons, much to his delight.

He looked up and smiled when they came in. Rhoda

hadn't heard them at the door over all the baby's noise. She startled when she turned around and saw them there.

"Oh, I didn't hear you there. So nice to see you, Veronica," she said. "Are ya *chust* out visiting today?" she asked.

Veronica and Aunt Wanda looked at each other wondering who should tell her first.

Veronica dove in. "Well, we're going on a little mission here. We'll tell you all about it."

Then Aunt Wanda suggested, "Why don't ya have a seat, Rhoda?" Then she bent down and taking his little face in her hands kissed the pudgy baby.

Rhoda obediently complied, almost worried by now. The coffee she'd put on wasn't quite ready yet.

Veronica began, "We're going to Canada tonight to visit Henry," she said, letting that sink in.

"Who is going?" Rhoda demanded.

Aunt Wanda replied. "Her and me."

Rhoda looked at Veronica and then Aunt Wanda. "Why?" was all she could come up with.

"We've been writing all this time and then got all sidetracked over the controversies in the churches, ya know, conservative old-time thinking, and modern stuff, and finally made up, and I think it's *chust* time now," Veronica summed up.

Aunt Wanda continued. "The bus leaves tonight and we are all ready. The van will pick us up here tonight, about eight-thirty. Isn't it exciting?" she asked, the idea finally sinking in.

"Are you two nuts? Have you lost your marbles? You can't *chust* show up there," Rhoda squeaked, horrified that they both must have drifted into some kind of delusion together.

"And why not?" Veronica calmly asked.

Rhoda was rendered speechless. She slowly got up and

chose three mugs from the drying rack by the sink. Putting those down on the table she brought the percolator with a hot pad to put it on and some cream in a little pitcher.

"So, can you stay for supper then? Nothing fancy," she asked slowly as if in a fog.

"Ya," Veronica agreed. "And we'll tell you all about it when we get back, I promise."

"Hm. Not sure what *Dat* will think about all this though," Rhoda mused while looking down into her coffee.

He who strikes the first blow confesses that he has run out of ideas.
- Amish saying

Part Three

The longer you put off doing a job, the harder it becomes.
- Amish School Motto

CHAPTER 24
Fruit Loops For Pigs

The van arrived right on time. Mrs. Dyck was their faithful driver. She had ferried Amish for over twenty years now. 'Hauled' is the correct word in the business. She had hauled Amish for over twenty years now. A Mennonite woman who had raised her children alone after her husband died, you could count on her to be prompt and perpetually happy.

Everything was an adventure to her. She thrived on her relationships with her Amish neighbors. She had been to Amish funerals and weddings, hospitals, barn raisings and out of state family reunions. Her customers paid her the going rate by the mile for trips, plus paid for her meals on the way. Often she had several hours to kill before the return trip, though not all trips wanted her to wait and return again the same day. On the jobs where she stayed until the wedding or funeral or whatever was over, she was often invited to attend the festivities. In this way, she felt honored that she had been giving a rare glimpse into their culture on so many occasions, more than most people.

Some would give anything to get a glimpse into this other world.

"Did I ever tell you about the time this one family had me drive by the Kellogg's cereal factory in Battle Creek, Michigan on their way home? They could get all sorts of cereal by the ton, practically, when you said it was for your pigs. It was seconds or something like that, but they give it away free. So, we stuffed as much in the trunk as we could —it's all in fifty-gallon garbage bags—and then they had me pass them the rest of the bags into the back seat so they could carry it home on their laps. I tell you, that car was stuffed to the gills. The last bags to go in were all Fruit Loops and before long I could hear them all crunching on the stuff! It was so funny," she concluded, laughing out loud.

After another few minutes she piped up again. "So, you're going on a little trip?"

"Yes," Veronica said. "We're going up to Milverton, Canada. In Ontario. It's about a twenty-six-hour ride on the bus."

"Wow. That's long," Mrs. Dyck marveled. "Have you been there before?"

"No," Wanda answered. "I brought my knitting."

"Are you staying long?" she inquired.

Veronica answered, "A week most likely. It's pretty exciting."

Mrs. Dyck had to stifle herself and try not to pry into other people's affairs. She had an insatiable curiosity, none the less. Finally, she inquired, "Family up there?"

"You could say that," Veronica said, not wanting to have to explain the entire story.

They arrived at the rural bus station fifteen minutes later. Four other people were milling around the station. They waved Mrs. Dyck goodbye and then purchased their tickets.

The evening was balmy so they sat outside on a bench to wait for the bus. A homeless man walked down the sidewalk and stopped by the bench asking, "Any spare change?"

Veronica answered, "No but I have a peanut butter sandwich and some cookies. Would that be okay?"

"Yeah, sure," he replied, very grateful for her generosity as she rummaged inside the carpet bag for the items. She gave him both.

"Thank you, ma'am. God Bless you!" he said.

"You too," she called after him as he walked away with his bounty.

Wanda looked over at Veronica. "That was nice of you. They tell you not to give 'em money. It only goes to drugs and drink. You never know, though, do ya?" Then she quoted the little truism, "There but for the grace of God go I," while shaking her head.

The bus left right on time. It was half empty. There were sleeping people sprawled across two seats up and down the aisle. Finally, they found two empty seats together and settled in for the long haul.

"I'm too excited to sleep," Veronica said.

"Well, I'm not, so goodnight, dear," Aunt Wanda said as she wrapped her woolen shawl around herself.

Veronica told her aunt then, "It's over six-hundred miles to Kitchener, Ontario. If we went by the way the crow flies, we could be there in ten hours. But this bus has all the meal stops—up to one hour each--then they have to switch drivers and stop at all the little milk runs through every town no matter how small on the way to pick up more people or let them off. Did you know after ten hours of driving time the driver is not allowed to drive again until another eight hours off duty? I guess they put them up in hotels along the way and the next bus or the one after that will be their next run. And they have to schedule all that for the entire country, and Canada too, I guess."

"Yes, dear," Aunt Wanda agreed with her eyes closed.

"Are you warm enough?" Veronica asked.

"*Chust* fine, *denki*," she replied. And with that Aunt Wanda fell asleep.

You can't sleep very soundly on one of these long trips, however, because every hour or even more often the bus driver will turn on his loudspeaker and blast the name of the next stop for his passengers' benefit. He certainly won't want someone to miss their stop and have to bring them into another town to get them back on yet another bus to the stop they missed.

The din kept up all night. "Maple Bluff" he'd shouted. Then "Monona, Burke, Token Creek, Sun Prairie, Bristol." Occasionally passengers would get on. At one point the bus driver had to wake up a bunch of those hogging two seats at a time to make room for the newer riders. They would grumble but no fist fights broke out on that trip, something that occasionally did happen.

While Aunt Wanda was still sleeping a woman who had just boarded the bus walked down the aisle and noticed them. She whipped out her phone and gushed, "Are you Amish?"

Veronica said yes, politely.

"Oh, you are so cute. May I please take your picture?" the woman asked, lifting up her phone. At that Aunt Wanda whipped her shawl up over her head.

"Well, no. We'd prefer you didn't," Veronica said.

The woman pleaded. Veronica smiled but didn't budge, just shaking her head. Speaking loudly to whomever might hear, the woman continued walking down the aisle then saying, "Well, I didn't know they could be so rude!"

Hardening of the heart is worse than hardening of the arteries.
- Amish saying

CHAPTER 25
Mamm is Back

It was midnight when the bus pulled into Kitchener, Ontario, Canada. They were the only ones getting off at this stop. The bus driver parked and announced a fifteen-minute break pointing out a Denny's restaurant across the street. Then he opened the cargo door below and hauled out their two suitcases.

"Thank you so much," Veronica said.

His reply was, "Good luck!"

I'll need it, Veronica thought to herself.

"Now what do we do?" Aunt Wanda asked looking quite perplexed.

"Well, we call the taxi company in town and get taken to the Swiss Inn. It's a cheap little motel where I made a reservation. We can sleep and wash up and be in better shape in the morning," Veronica explained. "I didn't want to get Henry or anyone else up to pick us up in the middle of the night."

"Gut thinking," Aunt Wanda noted.

They found the phone box in the bus station and called a cab. He arrived five minutes later and took them to their motel.

"Oh dear!" Veronica said when they arrived. "I just realized I only have American money to pay you. Is that okay?"

"No problem. Really," the young man said.

"Oh. Thank you so much," they both said. He drove off as they struggled with their luggage going up to the desk inside a tiny room marked, "Office."

"We have a reservation," Veronica told the girl behind the desk.

"Yes. Here it is. Here are your keys. Number five to your left," she rattled on. "Check out is at eleven o'clock. Complimentary continental breakfast in the room off to your right from six till nine," she said as she pointed out the room. "Have a good night!" she added cheerfully.

They dragged themselves with their belongings to the room. It was late, beyond late, but after being in such tight quarters with so many people neither one could imagine getting into clean sheets without a bath.

Afterwards, both quite refreshed, they slipped into the twin beds. Before she fell asleep, though, Aunt Wanda wanted to know, "What's a continental breakfast?"

"I don't have a clue," Veronica answered. "I guess we'll find out in the morning."

They were in the breakfast room at the Swiss Inn by eight the next morning. The offerings weren't anything to write home about, but enough to fortify them for the day ahead.

"Time to call a taxi," Veronica said. They were still at the breakfast table.

"Okay," Aunt Wanda agreed. "Aren't ya nervous?" she asked Veronica before draining her coffee mug.

"I'm petrified. I don't believe we're doing this. Now it seems utterly absurd, preposterous...even stupid," she said.

"No, it isn't. I think it is perfect," Aunt Wanda said. "It will totally disarm him, and you'll have something to tell your children and grandchildren and great-grandchildren about. It's terribly exciting. Daring, yes. Audacious, yes. But think what might happen," Wanda exclaimed with sparkling eyes.

"I don't want to think about that," Veronica countered, popping the last bite of her muffin into her mouth. She washed it down with some coffee before adding, "I'm giving the whole day up. He will have to take over. Lord, help us!"

"Amen!" Aunt Wanda said, though a bit too loudly she realized when several other Swiss Inn guests turned to look at her from their tables.

Veronica gave the address to the taxi driver when they were finally on their way, suitcases safely stored in the trunk.

The farm he took them to was sprawling. A huge main house with several additions attached to it, fanning out like the spokes of a buggy wheel in several directions. The scene of the paddocks was exquisite, idyllic even. Lush hay fields, sleek horses, and rolling hills beyond that. There were flower beds hugging the front and sides of the house and a freshly painted barn rising above it all.

The driver left, and the two of them approached the side door which they assumed was the kitchen entrance. Putting down their luggage and then looking at one another, neither wanted to be the first to knock. Before either could, the door flung open and three little girls silently stood there looking up at them. Nothing happened. Another minute went by, both frozen parties silently studying the other. Then the littlest of the three spoke.

"Mamm," she said and ran to Veronica, and hugged her knees.

Veronica knew it was futile to try to check her tears. She tried to peel the child off her legs and lifted her up in a proper embrace. The little one wrapped her arms around Veronica's neck, determined to never let this one go again. That was a nasty trick, getting whisked away thinking she'd never see her again. She whispered *"Mamm"* again into Veronica's shoulder.

In the hall behind the children, they could see a woman standing there, looking very perplexed.

"You're Veronica," she said. "I'm Edith, Henry's sister-in-law. We didn't get a letter saying that you were *kumming*. But maybe it got lost in the mail."

"It must have," Aunt Wanda agreed smiling sweetly. Of course there was no such letter.

"Well, *kumm* in. You must be exhausted. That is a long trip, for sure," Edith wondered. "Are ya hungry?" she asked as she reached to get the suitcases from just outside the kitchen door.

"No," Aunt Wanda assured her. "We stayed over in town and had breakfast. We didn't want anyone *kumming* to get us in the middle of the night. We're *gut* for now, *denki.*"

Rose would still not let herself be detached from Veronica's arms, so she sat down at the table and arranged the child on her lap. It was apparent that she was determined she was not going to let Veronica out of her sight ever again. Edith quickly switched into gear and put on the coffee.

Veronica smoothed down Rose's hairs and hugged her once again. "I missed you," she whispered into the back of the child's head. Rose half turned in her lap, smiled and patted Veronica's cheek with her little hand. Of course, the tears let loose once again. Aunt Wanda laughed.

"She knows exactly who you are, eh?" she said. "Let's hope Henry feels the same way."

"Me too," Veronica agreed, instantly nervous all over again.

"They'll be in for dinner in a couple of hours," Edith said. "This is such a surprise."

At that Rose wiggled off of Veronica's knees and ran to the great room. She grabbed her faceless doll and ran back, leaping once again onto Veronica's lap.

"Rosemary, isn't it?" Veronica asked. The doll had on the same color blue dress that Rose was wearing, right down to the black bonnet and blue pinafore that had blue buttons down the back.

"Ya," Rose agreed. Looking down at the much-loved, well-worn doll she told her dolly, *"Mamm"* again and nodded.

Veronica wiped her eyes once again with her hankie, stuffing it back into the sleeve of her dress. Veronica again picked up Rose and asked in Pennsylvania Dutch to show her where the outhouse was. Tucking Rosemary under her arm and grabbing Veronica's wrist in a vice, she pulled her through another door down the hallway and out to the back of the house.

Veronica wasn't sure if Rose intended to stay with her while she did her business or not. When they got to the outhouse, Rose let go of Veronica who went in and closed the door. Rose sat down on the top step and rested her back against the door, essentially making Veronica her prisoner. She settled Rosemary in her lap. She would guard the door in case Veronica had any plans to abscond at this point.

The soul could have no rainbows if the eyes had no tears.
- Amish saying

CHAPTER 26
Stranger Danger

"Can I help with dinner, then?" Aunt Wanda asked. "I'm useless as company. I need to be doing something with my hands, for sure."

"Oh, yes. I know what you mean," Edith said. "I'll get you the carrots and potatoes to peel," she said and laid the vegetables and the peeler and a bowl out on the table in front of the grandmother. Then, as an afterthought she brought her a cutting board and paring knife.

"Denki," Aunt Wanda said as she commenced the task before her.

Veronica and Rose were settled back at the kitchen table having washed their hands in the chore sink. The rest of the children migrated into the kitchen to check out the visitors. The last two of the siblings stood in the kitchen doorway between the great room. While they were sizing them up, the children whispered behind their hands to each other, commenting on the sight. None understood Rose's reaction to the younger of the two *fraus*. In fact, having grown up with Rose, they thought of her as a sibling, just one more member of the kid herd in their family. But she was calling this woman *'Mamm.'* They were perplexed and looked to their own mother who didn't offer them any explanation. It would remain a mystery for now.

They knew they all called Milo *'dat'* and they also called Henry *'dat'* like Rose did. It was interchangeable, it seemed, with *Oncle* or *Oncle* Henry. They just assumed this family had two *dats,* though none of their friends did. The other thing that had puzzled the children about Rose was that about a month or two or so back before the weather turned warm *Oncle* had whisked Rose away and they stayed away for over a week. They didn't know if they'd ever see her again. No explanation had been forthcoming. They grieved for the loss of their little sister, often asking themselves if perhaps she had gone to heaven. One other playmate at school had gone to heaven last year. He was killed in a farm accident. That left quite an impression on the other schoolchildren. Maybe something happened to Rose like that.

But as suddenly as she had disappeared, they woke up one morning and she was back, and very glad to see them. She couldn't tell them where she had been or the reason for the trip. She had met a lot of nice people along the way, she told them, and ate lots of cookies she could tell them that, but not much else.

So, things appeared to be back to normal as far as the little people were concerned. Her disappearance was soon forgotten, but now this. It was odd. Very odd. The other children couldn't figure out how Rose even knew this stranger while they didn't. There were often new people at church or when they went visiting on holidays, but they usually hung back until they got to know them a bit.

The children knew they could trust everyone in their district. That had been understood from the beginning. It was modeled after their parents' interactions with each other. They soon learned that everyone that looked like them and dressed like them and had hairs like them, and beards like their *dats* and dresses and *kapps* like their *mamm* was part of this wider family. Thus, it had been for generations. But then, one day that changed.

October 2nd, 2006, marked the day that all that changed. A school shooting in an Amish one-room schoolhouse in Nickel Mines, Pennsylvania left five children dead and five more in critical condition. These latter five all survived, though they are greatly impaired. The aftermath of this tragedy touched Amish worldwide and still affects many today.

Now children are instructed not to walk anywhere alone, never to accept a ride with a stranger, never to engage with an English person, be it the mailman or a lady out selling girl scout cookies, anyone. Some Plain communities have equipped all their teachers with walkie-talkies with direct links to the local authorities. Others have their own volunteer security shifts with Amish men taking turns patrolling school grounds and other Amish establishments. Sadly, 'Stranger Danger' is now part of Amish culture in America.

No winter lasts forever. No Spring skips its turn.
- Amish saying

CHAPTER 27

Lollipops and Roses

Veronica tried to get up from the table, but Rose would have none of it. Veronica held her hand and told her they'd stay together but she needed to get her suitcase just now. Rose clutched Rosemary under one arm and hung onto Veronica's arm with both of her hands. They slowly dragged the suitcase over to the sofa in the great room where Veronica opened it up.

She turned back her nightie on top of her clothes and removed the two packages she'd wrapped the day before they left. Handing the smaller of the two to Rose, she sat down on the couch. Rose looked at her while she held the gift. Veronica nodded, giving her permission to open it. By this time all the other children had crowded around them to see what was happening. Edith also came to stand by the children. Veronica looked up at Edith and asked, "is it okay if I give them a little treat?"

"Of course," she said. Veronica dipped her hand back into the suitcase and removed a little brown bag. She distributed the giant lollipops to each one of them. The children couldn't believe their luck. They'd never seen such big, round, multi-colored suckers in all their lives. A volley of *"denkis"* went up then. At the same time Rose had managed to unwrap her gift. She looked at it for a minute, turning the tiny dress over and touching the buttons on the back of the miniature pinafore. Picking Rosemary up she proceeded to undress the doll. Dressing her was more of a challenge but Veronica was right there to help.

Rose examined the results, first at arm's length. She smiled and nodded at Rosemary and hugged her doll to her chest in her new dress. Then Veronica passed the larger gift-wrapped present to Rose who exchanged it for Rosemary, giving the doll to Veronica for safekeeping. Veronica again gave her permission that she should open it, and Rose tore the paper off in one fell swoop, letting it float to the floor. She studied the dress there in her hands. Veronica detected a tiny smile before Rose nodded her approval of the gift. Crawling back up into Veronica's lap she tugged on her own pinafore, looked up at Veronica and said, *"effe"* (off.) Veronica unbuttoned her dress and pinafore, leaving on her undershirt and bloomers and helped her slip into the new dress. It fit perfectly, with even room to grow. Rose twirled several times to show it off.

The other children clapped their approval. Returning to Veronica's lap she whispered something into her dolly's ear. Veronica could not make out what she'd said, but the cheeky little smile was back. She knew Rose was happy.

The tears commenced cascading down Veronica's cheeks once more as she hugged Rose to her. *This has to work,* she thought to herself. *Dear Jesus, please, please show us the way. Help us to know Your will and take our hearts and our minds, and please tell us what to do.*

"Time to pick up the house before they *kumm* in," Edith announced to all present. The children instantly switched into gear and began collecting all the toys on the floor, first in the kitchen and then the hall and great room. They dragged the big wicker laundry basket along as they went from room to room, tossing in miniature farm animals and dinosaurs, wrapping paper and measuring cups, plastic ponies and dolls and books, sneakers and a hairbrush.

Lester looked up as they carried their treasures down to the bedrooms. He could see across the yard to the barn where Milo and Henry were securing the doors there. He dropped the basket and ran out the back door toward the brothers.

"Dat, Dat," he yelled. "We have visitors."

As they walked toward each other Henry yelled back "Who is it?"

"I don't know," he answered.

"Englische?" Milo asked, still walking toward him.

"No. *Amische*," Lester replied.

"Well, who is it then," Henry insisted.

"I don't know," Lester answered.

"Do we know them?" Milo asked.

"I don't know," Lester answered. "*Mamm* knows them I think."

"Are they staying for dinner?" Henry asked.

"I think so," Lester replied once again.

Then as they reached the kitchen door, Henry held the door for Milo who kicked off his barn boots. Henry followed suit. As he walked into the kitchen he called, "So who do we have...."

He stopped dead in his tracks. Milo walked up behind him jostling Henry. He too looked into the kitchen and just blinked. Henry was transfixed. His mouth open, his eyebrows furrowed as far down as they could go.

Edith spoke first. "The letter saying they were *kumming* must have gotten lost," she explained.

Aunt Wanda spoke next. "There was no letter. We *chust* came."

Rose looked up at her father from Veronica's lap and said only one word: *"Mamm."*

When Henry finally got his voice back, he asked, "How...why...I mean...when?" still not believing his eyes.

Edith answered for them. "They took the bus and got here this morning. I was as surprised as you are."

"But it looks like Rose is the only one who isn't surprised," Milo said.

At the mention of her name Rose looked up at Henry, smiled, and nodded once, patting Veronica's arm that was tucked around her middle.

"I didn't expect...I thought you were done with me...this is too *gut t*o be true," Henry stammered as he walked over to them and bending down enveloped both with his arms in a big hug, his tears falling on Veronica's *kapp*. The children stared at the spectacle, having only rarely seen any signs of affection in their presence.

Then Henry suddenly stood. "But we don't have to live in Canada," he raced to say. "We can go wherever you want. You *chust* say."

Veronica smiled. "We'll have lots of time to talk about it all. We aren't going anywhere.

"Kumm, sit down," she said as the children scurried around pulling chairs up to the table. One poured the water glasses; another one distributed the silverware while another was counting plates as she took them down from the hutch cupboard. Bread was sliced and little feet could be heard padding down to the root cellar to get the butter, pickles, and apple butter.

Edith and Wanda placed the steaming serving dishes on

the table while checking that serving spoons were already there too. Veronica was still being held captive and couldn't help with dinner, but she thought it looked like they were managing just fine without her.

Rose refused to slide off Veronica's lap to sit in the chair beside her where a place had been set. Instead, she carefully placed Rosemary on the chair after first spreading out the new dolly quilt on the seat. Veronica decided that was okay too, that she'd stop clinging to her once she knew she wasn't going to disappear again. They couldn't remain superglued together for the rest of their lives. She knew it would take time.

Everyone tucked in to the wonderful dinner. There were spiced beets with purple hard-boiled eggs, steamed vegetables with butter and chopped fresh parsley, baked beans, fresh corn bread and maple syrup. Bowls and platters and bread baskets were sent up and down the length of the long table. Henry's plate was full, yet he hadn't picked up his fork yet. Everyone else was eating. He sat looking at Veronica and Rose. It was the most beautiful picture he could ever imagine. His poor little orphaned daughter and his bride-to-be. He knew she would not have come all this way to tell him she was done with him. She had to have changed her mind, though he couldn't imagine how *Gott* had arranged such a miracle. He sent up a silent prayer then, *denki, denki, denki*.

"*Geendt*, Henry," Edith told him as she chopped up food in the little bowl on the toddler's highchair tray, though he was popping the morsels into his mouth faster than she could cut them.

Veronica looked at Henry. "We'll walk after dinner," she gently told him. "Eat now."

He obediently complied, though he didn't taste any of it. He was still in shock. That she would travel practically half a world away for him was beyond his comprehension, but here she was. He wasn't dreaming it.

Another silent prayer concluded the meal. Instantly the children popped up from the table and flew into action. They knew the drill. Dish pans were filled with water that had been already heated on the wood stove, the table was cleared in record time, leftovers tucked into the pantry to be brought out at the next meal to be used up, the table scrubbed clean, and the floor swept while the last dishes were being dried and stacked. Edith disappeared with the toddler to put him down for his nap. Veronica and Rose were still sitting at the table, though Rosemary was now carefully wrapped in her blanket and held in Rose's arms.

"I've got to get back to the barn. Can we talk tonight?" Henry suggested.

"Let's go out then, okay?" Henry said, coming around to the other side of the table and placing his hand on Veronica's shoulder. Addressing Rose in Pennsylvania Dutch he said, "Now you go play with the others." At that command she instantly grabbed Veronica's skirt with both fists, letting Rosemary fall onto the floor where she rolled out of her blanket and lay still looking up at them with her blank face.

Veronica explained, "She thinks I'll disappear on her again. I didn't realize how traumatized you leaving the States with her had been. She grieved as if I had died, Henry. She doesn't trust either of us yet. She'll need time. On another level she may have already been deeply affected when her *mamm* died, essentially abandoning her the first time. We just can't know all these things."

"I guess she's *kumming* along on our walk then, too. Huh.

I didn't realize. You think this'll ever wear off then?" he asked.

"I do. *Chust* give her time. Please. She'll be *chust* fine. I promise."

"Okay then. I'll see you for supper," he said.

"*Gut,* see you soon," she replied.

The afternoon went by in a flash. Veronica let Rose show her all her favorite haunts on the home place, that is as long as they were firmly holding hands. First were the goats, then the rabbits. Then the new piglets and the kittens in the barn. There was also the darling playhouse Milo and Henry had built the summer before. Rose chattered away as she narrated it all. Then they went out to the stream at the edge of the property. The other children then joined the little troupe along the way.

They took her by the bull pen on the way, two young studs frowning at the visitors from their side of the fence. "We don't sit on their fence," Lester explained. "Don't want to rile them up."

"No, of course not," Veronica confirmed.

"We aren't allowed to go to the stream without a grownup," Lester further explained to Veronica when they were almost there. "But you're here, eh?"

"So long as no one falls in, please," Veronica added to the conditions.

They collected dandelions on the way back to the house, filling the boys' hats and the girls' bonnets with them. They all sat at the picnic table near the stone wall that had a built-in grill behind the house, another project of the brothers.

They fashioned the dandelions into garlands that they

festooned each other's heads with, some humming or whistling while they worked. Veronica wondered at these happy children. Could she and Henry create such a happy home, too? Would they be blessed with so many? Would they all be strong and not come too early? *With* Gott's *help,* she prayed. *With* Gott's *help.*

It was soon time to wash up for supper. The dinner bell would ring soon. The children again knew their assigned tasks to set the table. Edith stood at the stove stirring a big kettle. Three bowls of Saltine soda crackers were spaced out the length of the table. A platter was piled high with cheese and ham slices. Next to that sat a bowl of Amish peanut butter spread and one of apple butter. Two baskets graced the ends of the table, a whole loaf of sliced homemade bread in each of the green and red-slatted handmade baskets.

I wonder if there are Swartzentruber Amish up here in Canada too, Veronica wondered when she noticed their trademark baskets on the table. They are sold wherever the strictest sect of Amish have settled. With farmland at a premium and competition with the English mechanized farms to compete with, cottage crafts have exploded in recent years. The baskets were the brainchild of someone who thought to give it a try, and it blossomed into a lucrative industry from there.

"Patties down?" Milo asked, prompting all at the table to whisk their hands into their laps for the silent prayer. Even the toddler got this one right, obediently closing his eyes.

Milo cleared his throat to signal the end of the prayer and the whole table erupted at once. Supper was not as formal as dinner in this house and the children were encouraged to tell about their day. It was often sheer pandemonium. They were all talking at once as they helped themselves to the food.

Edith stood at the stove ladling out large soup bowls that were passed down the table until everyone had one. Home canned tomato soup was on the menu, made from two of the last jars of it from the summer before. The soup shelf in the root cellar would soon boast rows and rows of gleaming jars once the canning commenced again in earnest. The crackers were passed around, each one crushing a stack of them with both hands into the soup before stirring them until they were soggy. There was no other way to eat soup in Amish homes.

Rosemary sat up in the chair next to Veronica. Rose was once again in Veronica's lap.

Edith spoke first. "Can't you sit *next* to her *daumling?*" she addressed Rose.

Rose wouldn't budge and ignoring Edith dug her hands into Veronica's skirt gripping her legs, too.

"She'll be sitting on yer lap till she's eighteen at this rate," Milo said lifting an overflowing spoon of soup and crackers to his lips.

"I doubt it," Veronica replied in English, not wanting Rose to be privy to the fact that they were discussing her. "We'll *chust* give her a little time."

Eventually the din settled down.

Reverting back to Pennsylvania Dutch Edith asked Veronica, "So when are ya going back home?" Rose heard that. Dropping her spoon onto the table she reached over to the vacant chair and grabbing Rosemary curled down into Veronica's lap.

Veronica looked at Henry. She needed an ally for this.

"Edith," he said, taking the hint. "Let's not make this

more than it is. We're gonna give her some time. I am sure it'll all work out."

Then Milo asked, "But what are you two planning? We don't have a clue."

Henry decided to drop the bomb then and there. "We're getting married as soon as possible."

The table went silent. Lester smiled from ear to ear and slapped the table with a resounding "Yes!"

The smaller children picked up on the vibe at the table and became frozen in place, not sure how to react to this news. They'd take their cue from the grownups on this one.

Veronica managed to get Rose to sit upright once again and settled Rosemary back in the empty chair.

"We'll go back together to the States—with Rose—and talk to the ministers. They'll announce the *banns* in church and give us the soonest date possible," Henry explained.

"But you're not going to wait till the fall?" Edith was horrified, ever the proper one, sticking to even the smallest rules and traditions.

"No, we're not," Henry stated plainly and resumed eating.

"Well, we'd like to be there," Milo said. "At least give us some warning, eh?"

"We will. I don't think it'll be big, being our second weddings and all," Veronica added.

"Where'll you live?" Edith wanted to know.

"We're working that all out. We'll let you know as soon as," Henry said. "Probably the States, though."

Supper over the family went into action once more. Dishes were washed, dried and put away while the floor was swept, and the table scrubbed down. Veronica appeared by the sink to help, her shadow glued to the back of her skirt by both hands while Rosemary was safely wrapped in her new quilt and tucked under an arm.

"Oh, youse don't have to help. You two go out and have a nice walk," Edith offered.

So the three of them went outside for a more intimate talk.

Rose passed Rosemary to Veronica to hold once they were outside and then took Veronica's hand. She reached out for Henry's hand with her free one. Rose was in the middle, just where she wanted to be.

"*Gut* thing she doesn't understand English yet," Henry chuckled.

"And what were you going to tell me that little ears shouldn't hear?" Veronica asked slyly.

Henry winked at Veronica then.

That one look melted Veronica's heart. She looked up at him. "I hope you know I love you to the moon and back," she said.

"I love you more," he answered.

A little girl becomes a young lady when she stops going through mud puddles and starts going around them
~ Unknown

CHAPTER 28
Out of the Mouths of Babes

When Rose became tired and couldn't walk any longer, Henry hoisted her up on his shoulders. Veronica was still cradling Rosemary on her arm. Rose looked down then and ordered them to hold hands. Henry looked at Veronica as if to ask if she was okay with that. She smiled her agreement to this new arrangement, so they held hands. Both felt it at the same time. They had passed into the next stage of this miracle. They both thrilled at each other's touch. They'd waited so long for this. They both thought back to the last weeks and months when they had doubted that their relationship would ever work at all. Definitely not to this level. Not now.

Both wished they would never have to let go. Henry's thumb caressed her hand, causing her to catch her breath. Love had returned, something Veronica had assumed was dead and gone.

Henry spoke first. "You really *chust* decided one day to *kumm* up here? *Chust* like that?"

"Uh-huh," she replied. "I guess I got tired of not knowing, of all the doubts and arguments in my head, ya know.

We'd both been on the fence too long already, don't ya think? I had to know."

"Well, I was beside myself," Henry explained. "Trying to figure out where I'd gone wrong, wondering if you'd had an accident. I didn't know what to think. It was driving me crazy, and I'd be no *gut* to you or Rose if I ended up depressed or worse."

At the mention of her name, the only part of the conversation spoken in English she had understood up to that point, Rose released her hold on his two ears and patted the top of her *dat's* head with both hands. He'd handed his hat to Veronica when he put Rose up on his shoulders.

"I don't think anyone can settle all the doubts before a marriage," she said. "That's what marriage is: working together when things do come up. You can't anticipate all of it beforehand and think everything will be all rosy after that. Well, welcome to marriage. You wrestle and struggle and argue, but if love is there, real love, it will see you through. You will find a way. You will be patient and kind and know it isn't going to kill you every time you disagree."

"You are right, ya know. Now I know why *Gott* sends us a helpmate. It takes two to take this on. We can't do it alone, or even fifty-fifty. It has to be one hundred percent each, eh?" he asked.

"My *dat* always said, more like two hundred percent each. You never stop trying or take it all for granted, I think," Veronica replied.

They walked on past the next farm, and under the boughs of a weeping willow tree that caressed them as they walked through its tickling curtain of leaves. Rose giggled at that. It was good to see her happy. He'd known she was asking about Veronica these past weeks. He thought she would just forget with enough time. He assumed she was happy for the most part, though she could be mopey at night, not wanting him to leave after their bedtime story. He doubted things were ever going to happen with Veronica back then. He was trying to forget, too. He was trying to convince himself it probably wasn't meant to be.

"I've been thinking, too, we've both been through this before. You'd think we'd be better prepared this time around, eh?" Henry asked.

"Well, I don't know. I think we're worse for wear. It's like we were so young and clueless before. We *chust* sort of rolled with the punches. And with *kinner kumming* along at the beginning there was no time to get all muddled with what ifs and buts," Veronica pondered.

"I know what ya mean. And now we're afraid of doing it all wrong, and afraid of being hurt again. Maybe that part never goes away. I don't know," he said as they walked along.

"My thinking is we'll be trying to figure it all out till the cows *kumm* home," Veronica said. "Aunt Wanda told me she thinks we should *chust* get married and get on with it. Be happy. Stop stewing."

"Really? Could we do that?" Henry stopped walking and turned to Veronica.

"I think I could," Veronica said, surprising even herself.

"I think I could," Henry hesitated. "Maybe we should."

"Okay," Veronica said, chuckling. "Have you ever heard of anything so *ferhoodled?*"

"No," Henry said laughing.

"Okay," Veronica agreed.

"Okay," Henry repeated. "I don't see any reason not to."

"Me either," Veronica said.

"Well then, we should make it official I guess," Henry said, getting down on one knee and putting Rose down between them on the grass. "Veronica, will you marry me?"

"If you'll have me, then yes," she answered. "What

Amische man does that anyway?" she laughed, swatting his shoulder.

"Hannes," Rose said first looking at Veronica and then her *dat*.

Henry stood up and took Veronica's hand once again.

"Do you get the distinct impression that Rose knows more about all this than we do?" Henry asked.

"Well, they say, 'out of the mouths of babes,'" Veronica recited. "Matthew 21:16 could not be any clearer," she added.

"Hmph," was Henry's response to that.

The three walked the rest of the way home.

When they got there, Veronica cleared her throat. "Um, I think we have a bit of a problem here."

"What's that? You haven't changed your mind, have you?" Henry asked sounding very worried, on the verge of panic.

"No, not at all. I'm *chust* thinking this little one isn't going to let me out of her sight now. What should we do about that?" she asked.

"Oh that. Well," he began. "There's the guest room in the main house. It's got a double bed. You two can go there and I'll be in mine in the *dawdi haus*. Would that be okay?" He suggested.

"Gut. That's perfect. Let's get her to bed first," Veronica suggested.

"We could visit then for a bit in the kitchen before we turn in. All this talking makes me hungry," Henry confessed.

Veronica laughed out loud.

"Shush! You'll wake the others, youse," Henry warned as he carried Rose up the stairs.

Trying times are for trying.
- Amish saying

CHAPTER 29

No Fair!

Once Rose was asleep, they both got up and headed for the stairs. Rose instantly woke up and began whimpering.

"Well, so much for that idea," Veronica stated.

"Darn it," Henry said dejectedly. He perked up then and said, "I know. I'll bring snack up here for us," and with that he bounded down the stairs two at a time.

Veronica sat on the bed next to Rose and stroked her hairs. She was soon asleep again.

"Will you ever forgive me?" she addressed the sleeping angel. "I didn't realize what we'd done by taking you away after that wonderful weekend. *Please, Lord, bless Rose and take away all her fears,* she prayed.

It still amazed Veronica how in love she felt, both with this little one and her *dat* besides. She'd lost both once before, a husband and a baby, and miraculously, beyond any of her wildest hopes and dreams, they were replaced, somehow. It was futile trying to make sense of any of it, but she knew it was true. Truer than anything she'd ever known. It seemed like a long time passed but eventually Henry came up the stairs, at a slower pace this time around, carrying a tray.

"Oh, this is nice," she said. He spread out a checkered tablecloth on the bottom half of the bed and set out pie, coffee mugs and all the utensils.

"Perhaps we are starting a tradition here, late night snacks when the *kinner* are in bed, ya think?" Veronica proposed.

"I don't think it'll always be on the bed. Hopefully, we'll graduate to the kitchen one of these fine days," he offered.

"Ya," she said with her mouth half full.

They talked late into the night. There was so much to say and so many plans to agree upon. Henry suggested they stay in Canada about another week so he could help Milo finish up the haying and all the other farm projects that couldn't wait. Then they would find an Amish boy or two to take care of the farm in their absence so Milo's family could travel back to the states with them for the wedding. They were banking on their minister back there agreeing to sort of accelerate the proceedings so Milo could get back to the farm before too much time had passed. They would invite the surrounding home district that Veronica belonged to but not the second and third cousins on their grandparents' side, twice removed. In other words, they were hoping to keep it as simple as possible. The children could miss a bit of school. They would be able to catch up quickly once they returned.

"We better get some sleep then," Veronica said yawning as she stacked the dishes and mugs onto the tray.

"I'll take it down," Henry offered. On impulse he bent down to kiss her. In response Veronica quickly turned her head causing the kiss to land on her cheek instead.

"Hey! That's no fair, now," Henry pouted.

"Too bad," Veronica whispered. "Your time will *kumm*," she promised.

Then she added, "By the way, it's 'not' fair, or it is 'unfair,' but not 'no' fair, teacher!"

"It's still no fair. You won't allow *chust* a little *shmuzzling*?" Henry pushed, though he knew it was futile.

Veronica only smiled in response.

"Now there is one thing I must tell you," Veronica said after breakfast the next morning on their way to the barn, Rose in tow.

"I know we can't have secrets from each other. Well," she hesitated.

"So..." Henry prodded.

"I know. Um, put on your seat belt, honey," she said.

He laughed, "Huh? Really? I don't think anything you say would surprise me," he answered.

"This will. Trust me," she added as she settled on a hay bale. Rose quickly arranged herself on Veronica's lap.

"This is an English-only conversation," she warned Henry.

"O...kaaaay," he replied warily, slowly lowering himself onto a hay bale across from her.

"So, what is so earth-shattering then?" he asked.

"Well, it's complicated, but I...uh, um...was given a million dollars from the family of the man whose car killed Amos." She let that sink in for a minute while he tried in vain to process that bit of information.

"This is a joke, right? I mean—" Henry asked. "This is your idea of a sense of humor?"

She continued. "The old guy shouldn't have been driving at all. It didn't kill him though, only Amos. He felt terrible, according to his wife who explained it all to us. It was all done perfectly legally. It's not as if we sued or anything at all like that. She said he wouldn't have any peace unless she could promise it would all go to us, me and the whole community when he died. Apparently, they were wealthy. Very rich. They left so much more than that to their own children in the will. I guess the property will also fetch a small fortune and go to them, too. The house has been in the family for over two hundred years.

"So, our minister went with me to talk to her and agreed it isn't like suing. We set it up at the bank so that if any Amish family needs money for surgery or to prevent foreclosure on a farm, or for a disabled child, then the bishop will approve of it and can sign it for me. He agreed with me that we don't want anyone ever knowing I had any part of it, but that it is *kumming* from the church. No one will know where the money came from. They'll *chust* think the bishop went around the district collecting donations for a family in need."

Henry couldn't speak. Finally, he shook his head and opened his mouth, but nothing came out. Veronica spoke next.

"I know it's a lot to take in. But the bishop and the minister who was in on it too were all happy in the end with the arrangement. But I want you to know about it and I don't want it going any further, please. Not your *bruder* or anyone. Promise me. I also really hope you are okay with how we're doing it." Then she was quiet.

"That is quite something, eh?" Henry said shaking his head. "No, I wouldn't have guessed that in a million years. Not at all. But if it is put to such *gut* use for the *Gemeeschaft*, then definitely, you did the right thing."

They sat in silence then watching Rose playing with the

doll in her lap, wrapping her and then unwrapping her in the little quilt.

"When might we be ready to leave, do you think?" Veronica asked him.

"I reckon by Saturday. Milo thinks we can manage it all by then. The Bylers have offered to watch the farm. They're *chust* up the road so it shouldn't be too much for them. All their *kinner* are pretty big so they'll all chip in," he said.

"It's almost getting real. I can't believe it. After all this time, eh?" she said.

She started to stand up to return to the house when Rose leaped into her arms holding Rosemary by a leg and wrapped her little arms in a vise around Veronica's neck, the dolly somehow also enfolded in the hug.

"Mamm," she said. Veronica was glad Rose couldn't see the tears falling onto her dress. She patted the little girl's back. "Ya, *mamm. Mamm* is back. Yes, *daumling.*"

We should always swap problems; everyone knows how to solve the other fellow's.
- Amish saying

CHAPTER 30
Blastoff

The home place was chaos while Milo and Edith packed for the trip to the States for Henry and Veronica's wedding. The Byler boys showed up to get instructions on how to take care of it all while they were gone. Henry and Veronica were busy putting in calls from the phone shack to the Greyhound station for bus tickets. They also called Amtrak hoping to find cheaper train fares, but Greyhound's prices were still better. Then, in the end they managed to hire a van and driver to drive them all the way from Milverton, Ontario to Veronica's home in the Midwest, their final destination.

The children definitely picked up on the festive atmosphere. They had never been on a trip of this magnitude. Milo got out an atlas and showed the children the route they would take and the places of interest where they might stop to see on the way. Edith was kept busy packing clothes for each child and making lists of what else she should bring. So far items like snacks, fruit, crayons and paper, comic books, magnetic chess and checkers sets and cards were on the list. The atlas would also accompany them so they could track their trip.

Her own stash of ginger root candy was on the top of her list. She baked ginger snaps for the children. The cookies had already proven their worth with the children on numerous, though shorter trips to stave off car sickness.

Rose was wary. Suitcases and knapsacks littered the house as the great escapade was being launched. She stayed close to Veronica, Rosemary tucked safely in her arms, Rose often nibbling on a cookie right out of the oven, though not ready for another disappearing act. She continued to accompany them on their nightly walks after supper.

Perched on her father's shoulders, while Veronica and Henry held hands they took to the back roads, using the time to catch up on what each one was thinking. They could cover a lot of territory in an hour or two, that way.

"Well, hello, you," Henry greeted Veronica as soon as they were out the door. "How was your day?"

"Busy for sure. I called Pennelope and Ruth today. Ruth was dead set against us *kumming* up here at all. You should've heard her!" Veronica said. "Pennelope got it, though. She was pretty happy that everything is working out." Then as an afterthought: "Well, Clara can back off now. Find some other poor widow to hound for the next decade. Sorry, I know that doesn't sound very charitable of me. You have no idea what she is like, though," she said chuckling and shaking her head.

"We'll have a lot to do to get ready for a wedding when we get back," Henry worried.

"Not really," Veronica answered as Henry put Rose down to walk for a bit. He took her hand, but she ran around the other way to hold Veronica's hand instead.

"You don't think this has gone on long enough? Are we *chust* giving in and spoiling her?" he wanted to know.

"Um," Veronica answered. "We need to switch back to English, but no. I think she'll need time to trust us. She isn't ready. She still thinks she might go back home, and I might not *kumm* with her, like last time. She's smart. Smarter than most I'd wager. I'm really sorry I didn't think what it would do to her when you left after our visit before. I had fallen in love with her back then, and she felt that. But then *chust* as suddenly I had dominated her life, *chust* as suddenly she was taken away from all of it.

"I was reading one of the books that Ruth loaned me on child development. There's something called 'separation anxiety.' It's a real thing, Henry. Most children go through it as a normal phase of growing up, like when they can crawl or toddle. They keep checking that you are still back there where they left you. Then they'll decide they are feeling secure and crawl a little further away. But disappear and it turns into fear. As their primary carer they depend on you for absolutely everything in their little lives. You are their whole world. Take that away and the world as they know it comes crashing down.

"They did a study, the book explains, with orphans in Russia. They were noticing some significant trauma in babies that were being adopted here in the states from Russia and the Ukraine. It turns out that they traced it back in every case to the orphanages who were so overworked that the babies almost never saw the same nurse twice. So they had no one person to depend on or bond with. Some then went on to foster care, where the babies tried to bond but their stay there wasn't always consistent, either. Some of those mothers worked and the babies went to daycare, meaning another set of caregivers, no continuity, and a lack of bonding. By nine months, the researchers found, the babies gave up trying to bond. They called that the 'threshold,' nine months. They basically turned inward emotionally. The *kinner* gave up trying to bond. It wasn't working. It seemed impossible. So you have profound developmental issues. They call it 'maternal-infant-attachment-deficit-disorder.'"

"Wow. That sounds terrible," Henry exclaimed.

"Well, it just sort of makes sense with Rose's being afraid I'll leave without her," Veronica explained. "I *chust* want her to feel safe and trust us again and I'm willing to follow her lead on this one. Let's *chust* take it one day at a time." Henry nodded in agreement, though he didn't quite understand all the technical jargon.

They walked together then in silence, listening to the birds on their way to barns for the night, and the cows mooing as they returned home to be milked.

"By the way, I'm thinking of the mountains of stuff we'll have to do to get ready for the wedding. Where do we begin?" Henry wanted to know.

Veronica laughed. "You won't believe this, but Pennelope has assigned herself the position to be our official wedding planner."

"What in heaven's name is a wedding planner, if I may ask?" Henry said.

"Well, there are people that you can hire to do all the planning, from soup to nuts, as they say. They'll supervise everything so you don't forget anything. They will order the flowers, send out the invitations, get the minister, help the wedding party get suits and dresses, order the cake, make name tags for the table settings, get centerpieces for all the tables. *Gut* thing we don't have bride's maids and groom's men and all that furor."

Veronica went on. "They will even take care of the gifts. It's the latest fad. It's called a 'registry.' I read about it in a magazine at the doctor's office a while back. See, she will write down whatever the couple is wishing for, and it all gets listed at like Target or Kohls, William Sonoma or some other fancy store. That way people won't give you four toasters or odd sets of dishes, but they can go to the store, and they'll check off the items as people buy them."

"That takes the cake!" Henry exclaimed. "That is perfectly crackers. Greedy too, *eh?*"

"I know. Anyway, Pennelope is organizing everything while we are up here. We won't need to do anything, and the sisters and sisters-in-law all have *bobbeli* so they don't have to do it all either this way. I think she is so dear."

"*Gut.* That is a load off my mind, for certain. *Chust* don't let her do that registry thing whatever it's called. That would be embarrassing, *eh?*" Henry said.

"Anything else on your mind then?" Veronica asked.

"It's not a big thing, but I'm thinking when we're married, we should start our day together, like morning prayers before breakfast, and again at night. I know most try to fit it in, but after a while, it goes by the wayside. I'm thinking we should really stick to it. I believe it will make all the difference. We need to keep our priorities straight, our eyes on the prize, the pearl of great price."

"Absolutely," Veronica concurred. "I *chust* want to make our home a happy place. It will take work but it's possible. More than possible."

They arrived again at the back door. Most of the lamps were out. Everyone would be in bed this late, with Milo checking the fires in the stoves and shutting down the dampers.

They quietly went upstairs and got Rose into bed. Henry sat on the bed humming to her while Veronica brushed her own teeth and got ready for bed, too. Rose was sound asleep by the time Veronica returned.

"May I kiss you goodnight?" Henry asked permission.

Veronica offered her hand to him.

"Aww, really?" he whined. "You're kidding, right? Ach! You aren't kidding, are ya?"

"*Chust* count the days now. We'll have the rest of our lives, years and years for all that," she pointed out.

He stood up and gave her a gentle kiss on the cheek. "You look lovely" he said softly, his voice a warm whisper curling into her ear.

Bibles that are coming apart usually belong to people who are not.
- Amish saying

CHAPTER 31
The Amish Wedding Wagon and Dirt Pudding

Pennelope could have been a corporate executive in another life, she was that efficient and organized. She'd contacted the Amish wedding wagon first and booked the date for three weeks away after consulting with the local minister who agreed to fast track this wedding, being a second marriage for both and the fact that some were coming from as far away as Ontario and needed to get back.

Leave it to Amish ingenuity. How do you prepare food for over three hundred wedding guests without electricity? Much less gather enough chairs, tables, stoves, sinks—you get the picture—with frequent weddings besides after the last harvest, November being the most popular time to get married. Well, the Amish have figured out a way to make the whole affair easier and more efficient. Enter the wedding wagon.

For those who don't know what a wedding wagon is, it is like an RV with a ramp added on, with six or seven propane gas stoves and ovens in it. Basically, a glorified food truck. There are also several sinks with hot and cold running water. Dishes, cookware, and everything you need for the food part of an Amish wedding come with the rental package.

There are also tables and a refrigeration unit. It makes it so much easier now than how it was even back in the 1990s. Back then you had to gather kerosene stoves from neighbors and families and set them all up in or near the wash house or buggy shed building. The family having the wedding feast had to get out all their dishes, utensils, glasses, cookware and then borrow from others to get the count up.

Pennelope took it upon herself to visit the family looking after Veronica's place and gained entrance to the house. The first thing she did was measure one of Veronica's dresses. Pennelope was taller than Veronica but basically the same size otherwise. A trip into town the next day, and she had all the fabric she would need for the bride's beautiful, teal-colored dress and cape. That same night she made a pattern from the old Cenex oversized calendar pages that were saved just for this purpose. In the morning, when it was lighter, she would cut out and sew Veronica's dress, getting most of it done the same day.

She picked up Sarabeth the day after that and put her to work cleaning the house. The neighbor boys were roped into cleaning the barn and yard. Pennelope brought Sarabeth back to Eli and Hazel's place in time to make them supper. This went on day after day until all was ready. The travelers wouldn't be back for three more days, Pennelope figured.

She was part of the single sisters' club and was excited that they had almost finished the quilt they had been working on together the winter before. It was a Double Wedding Band pattern. When they heard about the wedding they took a vote. It was unanimous, all agreeing it should be given to the couple. All new couples needed a new wedding quilt to start their life together and Veronica and Henry were no different there.

"Who's gonna make up the candy bags then?" Sarabeth wanted to know. Pennelope was driving her back to Eli's house after cleaning Veronica's home all day in preparation for the wedding.

"I forgot," Pennelope gasped. "I plum forgot."

"I could do it." Sarabeth jumped at the chance. "We're having a *youngie* singing this Saturday evening and I could get some of the other girls to help me. Eli would be more than happy for an excuse to go to Nordic Sales up the road tomorrow morning. I'll get everything we need. You can't have a wedding without the baskets of candy bags to give to your guests to thank them for *kumming*. The *kinner* would go on strike if that ever happened, no candy. Veronica won't have time to do fill all the bags, and she and Henry will be required to pass them before the meal. It's expected. You know they've nixed the celery, don't ya? But they can't leave out the candy, too."

"What about the *zellerich?* I almost forgot that also. Where's my head these days?" Pennelope moaned.

"*Ya.* That's what Hazel said, too. No celery. That'll be the first wedding of the century without it. Horrors!" Sarabeth shuddered and then broke out laughing. "Maybe the first time in all of *Amische* history, *ya* think?"

"We'll have all the other regular foods, I hope, or are they throwing that tradition out too? I've got all the food lined up, who is cooking what and all. *Roasht*—the Tom Betty Echs, noodles—Joel Enid Lehmans, mashed potatoes and gravy, I think I asked Norma Gingerich, pepper slaw...." Pennelope listed them off on her fingers.

"That is my favorite! Pepper slaw," Sarabeth broke in. "Who is making that?"

"It's in my notebook, Sara. I forget *chust* now," Pennelope said, quite frazzled by the enormity of her task.

"That leaves the rolls, pies, cakes, cookies and donuts. Are those doled out too?" Sarabeth wanted to know.

"I'm sure it's in my book. Oh, and tell Hazel to make some of her Dirt Pudding. Hers is the best. They really like that." Pennelope grabbed a pen from her apron pocket and wrote 'Hazel Dirt Pudding' on her palm. "I have to add her to the book, too," she explained.

"How much should she make?" Sarabeth wanted to know.

"*Chust* what she thinks she can manage," Pennelope said becoming unglued.

"The first time I saw that when I was little, I thought the gummy worms *kumming* outta it were real. It was *SO* gross. The pudding sure looked like real dirt, with all those crushed up Oreo cookies," Sarabeth laughed, shaking her head.

"I don't know what I would have done without you, Sarabeth. I really mean it," Pennelope said as she let out a relieved sigh. "I honestly mean that. I'd lose my head if it wasn't stuck on, ya know?"

Of course, Sarabeth smiled, so grateful for any praise. She had overcome so much and thrived on pleasing others instead now. She was genuinely happy and gave thanks every day for what God had done in her life.

Sarabeth's friend Ruth narrated the comings and goings of the last wedding she'd helped with last month while Sarabeth was off cleaning. When they finally got together again the next day she read it to her. She'd written it all down in her journal.

> *"The cooks in the wedding wagon are grateful for the cool breeze with six ovens going. They are chatting all at once, catching up about their families and community news. Today the bread is being made along with Peanut Butter pie. Two women are working on cutting the chicken leg quarters into two pieces. Daughter Naomi is washing all the bed sheets today. The clotheslines filled with sheets quickly dried in the breeze. There are small children playing together and the babies are being watched by the young girls. There was a large cooker of coffee this morning and delicious bars and snacks out on a table."*

"It is so exciting," Sarabeth told Ruth. "I can't wait. Less than three weeks now, *eh?*"

"I think you're right," Ruth replied.

"I think Pennelope has it all in hand. *Ya* think they're on their way home from Canada by now? I wonder how long it'll take to drive back. With *kinner*, I doubt they'll push on without stopping."

Onion skin very thin,
Mild winter's coming in.
Onion skin thick and tough,
Coming winter cold and rough.
- Amish saying

CHAPTER 32
*Watching The Radio**

They did stop after being on the road for about eight hours. They pulled off in Thunder Bay, Ontario before the border into the U.S. and found a quaint little diner. Before they left the van Milo set the children straight about what was expected of them in public. Eating out was a very rare occurrence indeed and proper manners were a must. Again, any talking was done quietly, and 'please and thank yous' were expected.

The waitress greeted the family and took them to a large table. She hurried off and brought back two highchairs for the two littlest ones. Passing out menus to everyone she asked what they'd like to drink. After taking their drinks order she left and returned shortly after with crayons and paper placemats for the children to color. Rose was the first to speak.

"Denki," she said addressing the waitress while opening her little box of crayons. Henry and Veronica smiled at each other. Of course, Rose was sitting between them. They had convinced her to leave Rosemary in the van so she could take a nap, the doll that is, which Rose agreed to.

Milo and Edith discussed the offerings on the menu and chose poutine, that rich, glorious Canadian mess of French-fried potatoes topped with steaming beefy gravy and squeaky cheese curds. Four orders of that plus a large pizza and corn dogs should feed them all. Ice cream finished the meal.

Renewed after such a special supper, the tired travelers found a roadside motel. They got two rooms, both with two queen size beds. The easiest solution for this crowd was designating a girls' room and a boys' room. The driver was in his own room. Showers were the next order of business.

The children got into their pajamas and jumped on the giant beds. Of course, the grownups were all tuckered out and anxious to get the children into bed so they could start early. The little people appeared to have gotten a second wind. After sitting all day, they had to let off some of that steam. Finally, Veronica came up with a plan. It was actually a bribe. She whispered it to Henry who passed it along to Milo. All agreed.

"What is that box thing hangin' in the corner over there by the ceiling?" Lester stopped jumping along with the little ones to ask. His *dat* answered, "Oh, that's a TV. Listen up. If youse all settle down and go right to sleep, we'll let you watch it in the morning. Okay?"

One by one the children got off the beds. Milo and Edith led night prayers with all on their knees. Then the boys and the two dats said goodnight and went through an adjoining door into their room. Lights were out in a matter of minutes.

At six sharp the next morning the boys returned to the girls' room and quietly sat on the carpet there. Veronica was up first.

"What are you doing up?" she asked rubbing her eyes.

"We wRuth see the box," they said, pointing to the TV.

"Hm," Veronica said, frowning, realizing they couldn't get out of this. One by one the girls and Edith woke up. The girls lay on their backs with the quilt pulled up to their chins. Rose left Veronica's side in her bed and crawled in with her cousins.

"Now what?" Edith asked Veronica.

"Well, there's a list of shows in that magazine on the dresser," she said heading there to pick it up. "Here it says 'Mr. Rogers'" she said as she continued to scan the page. "And, um, here it is, 'Sesame Street.' Channel two seems to be all the kid stuff," she said putting down the TV guide and picking up the remote. After fiddling with it for a few minutes it suddenly went on. The children's eyes were as big as saucers. Sure enough, there was Sesame Street, with Bert and Ernie and a dozen other puppets all chattering to each other. One of the puppets could even eat cookies. His name was apparently "Monster." The children were completely hypnotized by it. So were Veronica and Edith.

Milo and Henry wandered into the room through the connecting door just then, dressed and ready to go. They stopped inside the door and looked up. Soon they too were frozen in place and mesmerized by the TV. After a few minutes, Henry announced with a loud clap of his hands, "Okay, youse all. Five more minutes and we turn it off and get ready to go."

Of course, up went a volley of whines and pleas to let them watch just a little bit longer, but off it went. One of the little girls looked up at Edith while still tucked in bed with the blanket up to her chin and with dreamy eyes said, "Oh, *Mamm*. I *chust* LOVE the radio!"

Once they were back in the van, Henry announced, "I feel like pancakes for breakfast." At that pronouncement a resounding 'YES' went up from all. Henry had their driver look up IHop on their route south. The restaurant was close to Niagara Falls, so after an abbreviated visit to the famous waterfalls they made their way to the famous International House of Pancakes.

The visit to the Falls was cut short when a bus full of tourists from Japan began taking pictures of the Amish children instead of the famous falls. Henry tried to explain to them that he would rather they didn't do that, but it quickly became evident that English wasn't their second language... or their third or fourth for that matter.

Back in the van they headed to breakfast. After a very tasty meal they were all ready for the final leg of the journey. When they were on their way Veronica brought out her set of watercolor markers. She hoped this would entertain them for at least a little while. She started out by asking Rose what her favorite animal is.

"Glieder," she immediately responded. Veronica chose a dark gray marker and commenced drawing a kitten on the car window next to her. When it was done the children all clapped. Then the requests poured in.

"One at a time, please," she asked.

"Dinosaur" came from Lester.

"Hmmm. Would a brontosaurus do?" she said.

"Na. A Tyrannosaurus Rex" was his answer. Soon all the windows on both sides of the middle and back seats were covered in colorful drawings: Owls, penguins, dogs, ostriches, chickens, turkeys, guinea fowl, pigs, multiple dinosaurs, trees for the animals to sit under, a lake which looked more like a puddle for children to swim in. Passing cars started honking with people waving to them. Then one request came in that was quite unexpected.

"Me," Rose said, shyly.

"Okay. I'll try," Veronica answered. The finished picture was approved by all. Of course, then everyone wanted a portrait done.

"You did say that these markers wash off, right?" Edith asked nervously. *"Chust* checking."

Ever noticed how fast a fish grows from the time it is caught until the fisherman tells you about it?
- Amish saying

CHAPTER 33
Cloudy With a Chance of Meat Balls

The children were losing interest in the window drawings, and, frankly, Veronica was running out of window space to draw on. They still had more than six hours to go.

Rose had been listening to all the talk about going to a wedding. She had been wondering who was getting married. Most of it was in Pennsylvania Dutch, which she could understand, but then there were the long walks every night that were conducted almost exclusively in English which she wouldn't even begin to learn till she went to school in another year.

They were packing every suitcase they owned, it appeared. Now they were driving to the wedding. She had been so preoccupied with her fear of losing Veronica, that she had tuned out most of the discussions from the past week. She'd expressed her fears to Rosemary, her doll and constant companion, but Rosemary was unable to shed any light on the goings on. Were they going to a wedding and then leaving Veronica in the States where she'd apparently come from, when they headed back home? Just like what happened on her last visit. Or would she get to stay with Veronica when they all returned to Canada? Her father too? Was Henry going to stay with Veronica then, leaving Milo and Edith to bring home all the children back to Canada, her included? What were they planning?

No, she told herself. She couldn't bear that again. Just the thought brought tears to her eyes.

Time for the books, Veronica thought to herself. Everyone in the van was getting bored and testy. They wouldn't stop for lunch for at least two more hours.

"I brought some new books," she announced enthusiastically. "Can you all hear me okay?" she asked loudly. She now had everyone's attention as she opened the large carpet bag she'd taken out from under her seat. She'd visited the children's bookstore called, *The Wild Rumpus* in anticipation of this trip. She bought a few books that she was sure they hadn't heard yet. She'd read them to her classes when she was a teacher years ago now but doubted that they even carried them in the remote towns in Canada. She began reading. Rose sat next to her, leaning against her so she could see the pictures.

"*Cloudy With a Chance of Meat Balls,* by Judi Barrett. We were all sitting around the big kitchen table. It was Saturday morning. Pancake morning. Henry and I were betting on how many pancakes we each could eat." After each paragraph Veronica read, she would summarize them in Pennsylvania Dutch for Rose and the younger children.

She continued. "And Grandpa was doing the flipping." The vehicle was silent except for Veronica reading. She'd succeeded and got them fully hooked.

"Seconds later something flew through the air headed toward the kitchen ceiling...and landed right on Henry."

The morning seemed to fly by then. About noon Veronica whispered to their Henry, asking if he'd ask the driver to stop at a grocery store in the next town. Veronica ran into the store and came out with a large shopping bag. To save time she had decided on peanut butter and jelly sandwiches, which she could make in the car and pass out. Juice boxes, a couple of bags of pretzels and a bag of apples completed the meal.

After eating, the littler ones fell asleep, lulled by the hum of the van.

Finally, and all of a sudden, they drove into Veronica's farm.

Pennelope was there to greet them. Veronica called her from their lunch stop earlier in the day to let her know they were getting closer. Supper was on the wood stove and there were baskets of fresh sliced bread on the table. The weary travelers hauled in their suitcases and boxes. The children were introduced to Pennelope and then asked Rose to show them around the farm. Hugging Rosemary tighter with both hands she shook her head no. She would not leave the house. Milo asked her if she remembered the place to which she nodded yes.

"Then show the *kinner* around. Don't be shy," he coaxed. Again, she shook her head no.

Milo stood in the middle of the great room completely perplexed. He called out for Veronica who was already in the kitchen visiting with Pennelope.

"What the matter?" she called back. When there was no

answer, she went to see for herself. Milo pointed to Rose when she came into the room.

"What's the trouble?" Veronica asked Milo while looking down on Rose who was obviously in a snit about something.

"I dunno. Something's up. She won't take the *kinner* out," he explained.

Veronica knelt down next to Rose and asked her what was wrong.

Rose wouldn't talk or answer her.

"Are you afraid?" Veronica asked her, wondering at the child's body language.

Rose nodded. Veronica prodded farther. "You are afraid they'll take you away again? Without me?"

Rose threw herself at Veronica then, sobbing.

"There, there, Rose. No, you aren't going anywhere, and neither am I. You didn't know that though?" she asked. Rose shook her head no.

"You don't understand what's going on?" she pushed on.

Rose shook her head once again, wiping her nose on her sleeve.

"Well then." Veronica sat on the floor cross-legged and pulled Rose into her lap, giving her a hug.

"Well, then, Rose. I'm going to tell you a *wunderbar-gut* story. Okay?" Veronica asked. Rose nodded.

"Once upon a time, there was a *frau* named Veronica and a *dat* named Henry."

Rose looked up and smiled at that. She understood that much so far.

"So," Veronica continued. "They met and fell in love. They loved each other so, so much that they wanted to get married. You understand that so far, right?" Rose nodded and smiled.

"So they brought their whole family on a trip to Wisconsin where they got ready for the wedding. There was lots to do to get *redded* up. It was very exciting. Then the great day finally arrived. They went to church where all their family and friends met them for the wedding. At the end they were married. They lived in this very house then, your *dat,* you and me. And they will be a new family and they will live...happily...ever...after." Veronica waited a minute to let that sink in.

Then Rose spoke. "Is it true?"

Veronica nodded and hugged Rose tighter.

"And you are my *mamm?*" Rose wanted to know.

Of course, Veronica's tears made a grand appearance at that.

Rose frowned, not sure why Veronica would be crying.

"These are happy tears, my *daumling,*" she explained.

"And will you be my *mamm* forever then?" Rose asked.

Between wiping her eyes and blowing her nose Veronica managed to nod a resounding yes. Rose responded by throwing her arms around Veronica's neck. Just then Henry came back from checking the animals with Milo. As he stepped into the room Rose jumped off of Veronica's lap and ran across the floor toward him, grabbing his legs and hugging him.

"Dat, Dat!" she shouted. "We're getting married! Did you know?"

Henry looked over at Veronica who was trying to mop up a whole new waterfall of tears.

Veronica honked into the handkerchief then and could only nod and smile weakly.

"Well, I like that idea. Is that okay with you then?" he asked Rose.

"Oh yes," she replied. As she headed toward the door to

take her cousins on a tour of the farm, she looked down at her doll and told her, "Rosemary, me and Veronica are getting married. Isn't that *chust wunderbar-gut?*"

No dreams come true until you wake up and go to work.
- Amish saying

CHAPTER 34
The Wedding

Sarabeth sat between Pennelope on one side and Hazel on the other. Church was about to begin. They all knew it would be at least three hours if not longer on this special day. She leaned over to whisper to Pennelope.

"The second this is over I'm making a B-line to the kitchen to help." Pennelope nodded and shushed Sarabeth. She was so excited she could hardly sit still on the backless wood bench. Sarabeth twisted the hem of her apron and smoothed it out. And then twisted it again.

Sermons and hymns commenced, and then additional sermons and more slow, lengthy hymns, verse after interminable verse. Thus, the order of worship has been from time immemorial for the Amish Church. Since eons ago, the traditions of the Plain churches have been honored with very few alterations.

Halfway through what she guessed was the last hymn, Sarabeth leaned in toward Hazel and whispered in her ear, "When this is over, I'm outta here, full steam ahead...."

Hazel whispered back, *"Beheef du!"* her frown telling her

to hush. Taking Hazel's hand, Sarabeth turned her head back toward the front.

In front of the benches the couple were now standing facing the ministers lined up there. Rose stood between them. Rosemary was napping under the bench. The sermons were delivered in Pennsylvania Dutch, but portions of the service were conducted in Old High German, which Rose didn't understand yet. Finally, the marriage questions were asked.

"Can you both confess that God has ordained marriage to be a union between one man and one wife, and do you also have the confidence that you are approaching marriage with the way you have been taught?"

The couple both answered a resounding, happy yes.

Then Henry alone was addressed.

"Do you also have the confidence, Brother Henry, that the Lord has provided this, our Sister, as a marriage partner for you?" to which he said an enthusiastic "yes!"

Then Veronica was asked, "Do you also have the confidence, Sister Veronica, that the Lord has provided our Brother Henry as a marriage partner for you?"

Veronica also confidently answered yes.

The next question was asked of Henry,

"Do you also promise Veronica that if she should become in bodily weakness, sickness, or any similar circumstances and in need your help, that you will care for her as is fitting for a Christian husband?" to which he again said yes.

Again, the presiding minister asked Veronica, "Do you, Veronica promise your husband Henry the same thing, that if he should in bodily weakness, sickness, or any other similar circumstances need your help, that you will care for him as is flitting a Christian wife?"

Veronica answered yes.

Then the minister asked the couple, "Dear Ones, now

we have the important question of the Church. Do you promise together that you will come with love, forbearance and patience to live with each other, and not forsake the other until God will separate you in death?"

Again, both answered yes.

A moment later a tiny 'yes' could be heard as it was added to theirs.

Of course, the minister didn't instruct the groom to kiss the bride. There was no exchange of rings, no honeymoon. Just a God-centered marriage, surrounded by family and friends where two people join as one to start a life where both are tasked with leading the other to God. Then the minister brought their hands together and laying his hand on top, gave the final blessing.

As the ministers filed out first, the men rushed to set up for the feast. The tables were put in a horseshoe-shape, placing a special one known as the *"eck"* in the corner for the newly married couple to sit and eat at. The wedding party was directed to the tables placed adjacent to the *eck*.

Since there are so many guests at Amish weddings, food is often served in shifts. People sit down, enjoy their food, and leave the table. Then the helpers clean the tables, wash dishes, and set up right there at the tables for the next wave of guests.

After this, the first meal, the guests gather around to sing hymns.

Afterward, there will be a time where single boys will have a chance to pick a single girl as a partner for the rest of the evening's festivities. The two will sit next to each other during the second dinner. In some communities the newlyweds have fun doing some matchmaking, picking and assigning these partners themselves.

Toward evening the second meal will begin. This time older guests and the parents of the newlyweds are served first. The food is a little different, but guests will likely eat stewed chicken, sweet potatoes, macaroni and cheese, cold cuts, and more Amish desserts. Then everyone will continue socializing until it's time to head home.

"I pray that Benuel chooses me to sit with him at the table," Sarabeth confided to her friend Ruth.

"There are for sure plenty of *youngie* here," Ruth observed. Both had been asked to help with the table serving and cleanup for the wedding feast.

"Who are you wishing will ask you?" Sarabeth asked. "I could always let him know and *chust* say a little bird told me."

"Well, I don't want him thinking I am after him," Ruth answered, sounding very concerned. "That could ruin any chance of ever getting to know him."

"Who is it though?" Sarabeth wanted to know.

"Wayne Mast. But you can't tell him who told you. Promise?" Ruth nervously told her friend.

"Leave it with me," Sarabeth assured her.

Be life long or short, its completeness depends on what it was lived for.
- Amish saying

CHAPTER 35
Purple Eggs

Milo's family were staying with a cousin nearby until they would travel back to Milverton, Ontario. The plan was they'd come over later in the day to hang out and let the children play, probably leaving after supper.

Henry guided the horse up to the barn when they got home after the wedding. Rose was asleep on Veronica's lap. Henry jumped down from the buggy and ran around to the passenger side, lifting Rose up and taking her inside. She didn't stir. Veronica got out of the buggy and unhitched the horse. Then she brought her into the barn and secured the horse in her stall. Glancing around everything else appeared in order inside the barn.

She walked back to the house, letting herself into the kitchen and lit a lamp there. Exhausted from such a long day, she could only formulate the tiniest of prayers as she looked around the room, her heart swelling with love and gratitude.

"*Denki, Gott. Denki* for how you take care of us. *Denki Yesus...*" she whispered. Then she thought, *my life will never be the same. A whole new time for certain.*

Then thoughts of the coming night flooded her mind. It wasn't fear. It was just the unknown. Yes, she had been married once, but it was as if she hadn't been. This love was different. More mature, perhaps, after both had been tried by fire. The Song of Solomon popped into her head at that moment. *Let him kiss me with the kisses of his mouth: for thy love is better than wine.... Yes,* she thought. *I will let him kiss me....*

"She didn't even wake up," Henry whispered his report coming back down the stairs.

The next morning Veronica tiptoed out of the room and went downstairs to stoke up the fire box and start breakfast. *Our first ever breakfast...*she mused. She got the coffee percolator on the stove and gathered all the other things she'd need. As she cracked eggs into a bowl she heard the pitter patter of little feet. She smiled. *I'm a* mamm. Of course, those pesky tears returned in full force. Rose snuck up behind her, Rosemary in tow, and shouted "BOO." Veronica spun around and picked Rose up in a huge hug, setting her down on the counter.

"You sure look happy, *liebling.*"

"We're married! That's why." Rose shouted back, her grin from ear to ear.

"You and me!" Rose continued.

"And *Dat,* too," Veronica added. She'd been wondering what had been going on in that little head.

"Is that true?" Rose asked, suddenly solemn.

"Yes," Veronica explained. "You and me *and Dat.*"

The child frowned as she tried to process that thought. Then she nodded once and looked up at Veronica. "Okay," she said, as if they needed her permission for the arrangement.

She helped stir the eggs and counted out bananas for the table. Then she set the places as good as any four-year-old could. The silverware ended up on opposite sides and one place received two forks, but no one would mind. Especially not today.

"Okay," Veronica pronounced. "You go get dressed and then I'll do your hairs. Don't worry about the buttons. And tell *Dat* to *kumm* down. It's almost ready." Rose nodded once and ran to the stairs.

When the two stragglers finally came into the kitchen, Henry looked at Veronica as she buzzed between the stove and the counter preparing breakfast. She turned then and saw him sitting at the table watching her, with Rose on his lap where she was fussing with Rosemary's blanket. He winked at her.

That one look melted her heart. She blushed and stifled a laugh. That made him laugh, that one wink could disarm her like that. He laughed until he had to wipe his eyes on his shirt sleeve.

"Are those happy tears *Dat?*" Rose asked him. He nodded and hugged his little daughter.

Yes, marriage is funny, Veronica thought to herself. *Such a mystery, really.* Gott, *You sure have a sense of humor.* She laughed out loud again.

Henry coughed and cleared his throat to compose himself and asked, "So what is the first order of the day?"

"Did you forget? We have to visit all the people who came to the wedding and left gifts and thank them, even if it takes all week. Pennelope is already on it. She wrote down the name of each family, their address and what gift they gave us. Otherwise, we'd never be able to get it all straight.

"We really have to do that? Darn. We did it the first time we got married. Oh well. If we must," he said dejectedly. "At least our wedding planner knows what to do."

"Can I *kumm* too?" Rose asked.

"Of course," Veronica said. "You won't get out of it either," she told her sternly.

Rose only laughed. This married thing sure was fun.

Edith and Milo and their tribe came over toward supper time. Edith got right to work fixing supper for the crowd. Henry and Veronica and Rose weren't back yet, having a whole page of names of families they still had to visit.

"It's gonna get dark soon," Henry said, examining the sky. "Might rain. I say we go home and pick it up again tomorrow."

"Fine with me," Veronica said.

"Fine with me," her little shadow echoed, making Henry laugh. "I don't know if I am ready for this, living with two opinionated liberated women."

"You're doing *chust* fine," Veronica noted.

Again, Rose repeated, "You're fine, *Dat.*"

When they drove into the yard, they could see the cousins all running in a game of Shadow Tag, or something. Rose hopped out of the buggy once it stopped and ran to join them.

"She isn't so clingy, have you noticed?" Henry asked.

"I know. I am so thankful. I think we've moved out of that phase. That was rough, eh?" Veronica asked.

"Sure was. It makes sense, though," Henry observed. When they got to the kitchen, they greeted the cooks there. Edith had Milo stirring something on the stove while she pulled a tray of biscuits out of the oven. Saltine crackers in wax paper sleeves were laid out on the table and the places were set. Apple butter, sweet Amish peanut butter, and purple eggs and beets completed the meal. Practically a staple in every Amish home, pickled hard boiled eggs and beets often show up at a meal. The cooked, peeled eggs are added to the beets and brine and quickly turn a beautiful purple. The eggs keep longer that way, too.

"It's all ready. *Dat,* would you call in the *kinner* and supervise hand washing please?" Edith asked Milo.

"I couldn't eat another thing if I tried," Henry stated. "We had to endure twelve snacks today. And we have to do it again tomorrow. I'll burst!"

"Me too. Of course everyone wanted us to *kumm* in. And they all baked, for sure. We ate scones and cookies," Veronica began listing the snacks.

Henry continued, "and pies and cakes and *kaffi*...."

"And here is a banana loaf Tabatha sent home with us. You can put that out tonight too," Veronica added.

"And more *kaffi*..." Henry groaned.

"Well, youse two *chust* come to the table and tell us about your visits today." Milo said as he watched the line of children washing up at the sink. "Ya don't have to eat anything," he added. "I remember ours the day after the wedding," he chuckled. "And we didn't have a clue about any of these critters," he said, indicating the children with a sweep of his arm.

"We never really know what the future holds, eh?" Veronica thought aloud. She looked at Henry again as she sat down. Again, he winked. "Stop that!" she silently mouthed, frowning. She was already blushing again.

Since this was Henry and Veronica's house now, and he was the head of the new family, the honors fell on him to conduct grace. When all the children were there, he asked simply, *"Patties down?"* They'd all been trained in Amish table etiquette since they were big enough to sit in a highchair at the table. All the little hands flew beneath the table and onto their laps, eyes tightly shut. Only when *Dat* cleared his throat signaling the end of the silent prayer could they open their eyes and relax.

Too many people during the first half of their life spend health to gain wealth. During the second half, they spend wealth trying to regain their health!
- Amish saying

CHAPTER 36
Worry Ends

After a hearty breakfast the next morning, Henry, Veronica and Rose went to the cousins' farm where Milo's family had been staying for the wedding. They crammed everything into the buggy, children sitting on grownup's laps or on the floor behind the benches but on top of suitcases and backpacks. Edith held a giant picnic hamper on her lap with their lunch. They'd decided to take the Greyhound bus back, since this time they were less people, Veronica, Henry and Rose staying behind.

They got to the bus station in plenty of time. The bus wasn't even half full, which was a relief since the parents weren't too keen to have any of their children sitting with strangers.

The cousins all hugged each other goodbye. Rose walked over next to Veronica on the loading platform and grasped her hand.

"*Mamm,* I'm sad," Rose told Veronica dejectedly.

"Whatever for?" Veronica asked surprized, completely taken aback by this pronouncement.

"They are all going home. They're my friends," she told her mother tearfully.

"I know. But they will visit here again, and we'll even go to Canada to visit, maybe at Christmas. Won't that be fun?"

"I suppose. Yes, I guess," Rose answered.

"Let's ask *Dat* if we can visit for Christmas, *eh?*"

"Okay," she answered.

They all waved goodbye until they could no longer see the bus speeding down the highway. Returning to their buggy Rose popped the question when they were all seated on the bench. "*Dat,* can our family go to Canada for Christmas? Please? Huh?" Rose begged.

Henry looked over at Veronica, his look asking where this came from. She nodded back.

"Well," he began. "That is a really *gut* idea there, Rose. I'm glad you asked. We'll plan on that and see if we can do it, okay?"

Rose nodded and leaned against Henry where she quickly dozed off.

Then in English he addressed Veronica. "Where did that *kumm* from anyway?" he asked.

"She was sad saying goodbye to the *kinner,* thinking she'd never see them again," she explained. "Maybe by Christmas that might work out, *eh?*"

Henry answered, "Well, if hell don't freeze over and the creek don't rise, as they say...."

They chatted all the way home. It was only their family now in the house. *A new time. Such a blessing. All of our fretting and disbelief. Lord, help our unbelief going forward now. Of course, Gott could fix it all,* Veronica told herself. *I wasted so much time and energy. Worry ends where faith begins, they say. It's true. And what does the future hold now? I guess time will tell.*

The lamps all extinguished, and the house closed up for the night, they knelt by the bed for night prayers together.

"Our second night together," Veronica said as they got ready for bed.

"You going to count them each night then?" Henry teased.

"Ya, one thousand, seven hundred twenty-two…" she teased back. Then she was more serious. "You know, He does really wipe away every tear."

"*Kumm* here," he whispered, gently enfolding her in his arms. She rested against his chest. *So strong, so* gut… she told herself as she wrapped her arms around his waist and melted against him.

"My love," he whispered. "Thou hast ravished my heart my sister, my bride," he said before bending down and kissing her. Then he continued, "Thou hast ravished my heart and given me courage with a single glance," he quoted the Old Testament.

"I love you to the moon and back," she whispered in his ear.

"I love you more," he whispered before the next kiss.

She opened her mouth to say something more when he said, "Hush…."

The End

"God speaks quietly, very quietly but He does speak, and He will make known to you what He wants you to do."
~ Catherine Doherty

Available Winter 2024
Merry Amish Christmas
The final book of The Amish Veronica Series

Turn the page for a sneak peek!

Merry Amish Christmas

Chapter 1
KAFFI SOUP

"*Mamm! MAMM!*" The shouting could be heard throughout the whole house.

"*Maaaaammm!*"

"What is it, for heaven's sake?" Veronica called back from the kitchen sink. She wasn't sure yet where it was coming from, but she had a good guess who it was. She could hear the old wooden stairs creaking as little feet bounded down them.

"Let's make *Dat* Shoo-fly pie for supper. Okay?" four-year-old-soon-to-be-five Rose called as she ran into the kitchen and stood barefoot in front of Veronica in her muslin nightie buttoned up to her chin, her waist length brown hairs covering one eye and most of the other one also.

"And corn noodle soup, too. Pleeeeeease," she begged, her hands tightly clasped in front of her as if in prayer.

"Oh, my goodness, *daumling*. He will get absolutely *geblumpt* if we keep making him pies every day," she said.

"Oh, but we need to keep him happy, eh?" the little girl asked. "And you promised to teach me how to make it," she said, reminding Veronica of this fact that was as good as a binding legal contract in her little mind.

"Well, we'll see," Veronica said, taking in the little hands. "I have to make breakfast first. Then we'll see what we have for today, that is if that meets with your highness' approval," Veronica explained. "You have your chores before you eat, don't forget. Open their pen on the *hinklehaus* and scatter the chicken feed first. Then bring in all the eggs. There should be plenty today. Take your basket when you go. Go and get dressed and I'll do your hairs first," she added. With a nod of her head, and content that her prayer would be answered, the little sprite turned and was gone.

It had been six months since the wedding. My, but what a fine wedding it was, too. Maybe a bit grander than her first marriage even to Amos. Everyone was genuinely glad for Veronica and Henry, especially after all the hardship both had been through, first losing her tiny preemie baby and then Amos being killed in a buggy accident hardly a year later. That old guy driving the car was in his eighties, for goodness' sake. He never should have been driving that big fancy car at all. He ran one stop sign. Just the one, but that's all it takes.

Henry had not escaped tragedy either. He and his young wife couldn't have been happier as they expected their first baby. No one could have imagined the complications that arose leading to her death. Little Rose survived the ordeal, though that seemed insignificant consolation to the bereft father.

Veronica had already been up for two hours. She was dressed in her favorite sage green *tract*, with her kitchen apron over that. She'd begun making a matching dress for Rose out of the same cotton-polyester cloth. Just enough polyester that she didn't have to iron it every time she washed it. Hanging on the clothesline whipped all the wrinkles right out of it. It was also cooler in the summer months. The heavier fabrics were more suited for cold weather, worn over your thermals or a wool slip.

Her white starched *kapp* was already pinned in place over her tight, dark brown bun. She too was barefoot. Your feet toughen up when you only wear shoes for church or town trips. It also helps keep the floors clean if you aren't dragging in all sorts of dirt on your shoes every time you come into the house. You didn't worry as much putting toddlers down to graze on the floors either. Hopefully, the number of germs from the barns were reduced there, too. Mind you, a certain amount of exposure to some germs built up one's immunity to the environment.

The children loved being barefoot for the greater part of the year. If there wasn't frost on the ground, you'd find them barefoot, even in church or at school. That has an added benefit of saving literally tons of money on shoes for growing children. Stubbed toes and scraped knees were their lot no matter what they were or weren't wearing on their growing feet.

Veronica continued crumbling the day-old Southern Gal Biscuits into three bowls. Any bread would do. She saved all the crusts and heels of the bread in a bowl in the warming oven on the wood stove to dry out. There was so much you could do with old bread. Bread puddings, a binder for meatloaf, a fondu supper, breakfast *mosch*, a thickener for soups, herby croutons for salads or Haystack suppers. The list went on. If you were out of bread or biscuits, you could always use crushed Saltine crackers for the breakfast kind. Homemade Grapenuts would work too. Rose claims that they should try popcorn in it sometime.

Veronica moved the scalded camel milk away from the hottest side of the wood stove. She measured out three tablespoons of instant coffee into the pan and stirred that into the hot milk, careful not to let it boil and burn. She stopped then, spoon frozen between the bowls and the coffee canister and closed her eyes to breath in the rich coffee smell. Veronica loved this time of day. So silent, waiting for all the earth to awaken once again which it did every single day without fail. How did God do that, anyway? Would the ritual ever end? In Eternity perhaps?

Looking back to what she'd been doing, she measured out three tablespoons of raw honey or occasionally brown sugar, stirred it gently and it was ready to pour over your biscuits or bread or crackers. Adding a spritz of almond extract or a dash of cinnamon is optional.

She had discovered camel milk only a couple of years ago. It is the perfect solution for those with lactose intolerance. An Amish fellow in Missouri has a herd of camels that he milks and sends it all over the country. A mama camel will only let down her milk if her calf is in the pen with her, Veronica had read.

The sun was just coming up and peeking into the kitchen windows. Veronica reached up above the table, cranked down the wick on the mantle lamp that was hanging from a chain in the ceiling and blew the flame out.

Rose would be starting school in the fall. Henry and Veronica decided recently to try speaking only English at home to help Rose make the transition to English easier. Amish children don't learn English as a second language until they attend school. Before that they only know *Pennsylfaani* or Pennsylvania Dutch.

Rose came back into the kitchen to have her hairs braided. Sitting at the kitchen table, swinging her legs that weren't long enough yet to touch the floor, she hummed as Veronica brushed and then braided her hairs. Then she rolled it all into a bun and secured it with stretchy bands. Her black cotton kapp tied under her chin completed the morning routine. Hopping off the chair she ran barefoot to the mud room and grabbed the egg basket hanging there. Then she stopped, spun around and ran back to the kitchen throwing her arms around Veronica's middle, the wire egg basket hitting her mother squarely at the back of her knees.

"So, what's that for?" Veronica laughed as she hugged Rose.

"*Chust* because I love you sooooo much, *Mamm*," came her answer.

"Oh. I see. Well, I love you more," Veronica replied, hugging her back, wishing she didn't have to ever let her go.

"Oh, no you don't," Rose answered.

Then more subdued, she stood back a step and looked up at Veronica.

"Tell me about my first *mamm*, please?" she asked.

"Oh, well, then," Veronica began. "Get the eggs first and then let's sit down here for breakfast *daumling*."

"Okay," Rose agreed as she skipped toward the back door.

Suddenly Veronica called her back. "*Kumm* here, youse," she demanded.

"Huh?" Rose questioned, noticing the firmer voice this time. She froze in place. "Would you please tell me, Missy," Veronica began, trying not to explode quite yet.

"What is that on your toenails?!" she demanded.

"Well," Rose began," aware that trouble could be brewing just now. "Ya know last time we were at the farmers' market? Well, I saw all these ladies with painted toes *kumming* out of their sandals. So I wanted to try that," she confidently stated.

"But what did you paint yours with? Why?" Veronica asked, no closer to understanding the little girl.

"I got the magic markers on *Dat's* desk," she explained, not too worried yet that this might spell consequences.

"Ya know, those are permanent, don't ya?" Veronica said, quite horrified at this point.

"But I thought they looked pretty." Rose figured this was a perfectly good explanation.

"Um, no." Veronica said. "We don't paint ourselves or wear makeup or jewelry for a reason, my dear," Veronica answered, allowing for the child's innocence.

"*Gott* gave us our bodies to be His temples. We don't have to adorn ourselves. That's vanity. That's what the world does, *daumling*," Veronica explained. "All that makeup, jewelry and nail polish does is attract attention to ourselves. That is a sin." Veronica had not imagined she'd be having this talk with her daughter this early. She was barely five, for pity's sake.

"Oh," was Rose's reply. She would have to understand this better. Perhaps later.

Henry had also been up early when he first heard Veronica puttering around the kitchen, pots clinking, the wood box on the old black iron stove being shaken to distribute the few hot coals there that had survived the night. Then he could hear a log being jiggled into place over the coals and the little door slamming shut on the wood box. Then the squeak of the rusty old damper being cranked open.

By the time Henry dressed, Veronica already had 'first breakfast' ready for him. A large tankard of strong coffee loaded with cream and sugar was the perfect thing to get you up and running on a brisk morning. He stood by the stove gulping the first swig of coffee. He'd carry the large mug with him to the barn. Eyeing the cookie jar on the shelf above the stove, he contemplated taking along a handful with him. Seeing his eyes looking at the cookie jar Veronica spoke up.

"Sorry it's empty," she stated. "We're hopefully making more later today."

"Maybe Monster cookies? Or your Dunkin' Snaps" he suggested. Then he added, pushing his luck even further, "or both?" he asked meekly, looking over the top of his mug as he consoled himself with another large swig of his coffee. His tousled curly brown hairs looked almost comical atop the lean face. He'd tried all during his teen years to get them to lay flat, even resorting to wearing a stocking cap to bed after he'd wet it all down. It was a hopeless cause.

His clean shirt didn't hide the strong physique, his arms filling out the sleeves and his shoulders almost straining the fabric in back. Black leather suspenders were buttoned front and back at the waist of his barn door trousers. Still barefoot he took a step closer to Veronica. He leaned in, careful not to splash hot coffee on her, to plant a coffee-flavored kiss on her lips. Then he turned toward the door to put on his Wellington barn boots, these days called 'Wellies' for short.

"See ya soon," he called over his shoulder as he pushed open the door, his gray eyes twinkling with thoughts of all kinds of mischief. Then he winked at her. That was the one thing that always made her blush. Even after all these months. With that the kitchen door banged shut with a thud and she returned to making second breakfast, which would happen when they were all at the table, the first chores done.

Almost two hours later Henry was returning from the barn and his morning chores. He shook off his barn boots at the mud room's jute rug and hung up his straw hat on a peg in the hall, leaving his hairs plastered to his head with sweat. He pulled up his barn door trousers and tucked his shirt back down into the pants. His sleeves were already rolled up.

Walking to the chore sink by the door he opened the spigot on the gravity water tank and washed his hands with the fragrant homemade soap. Grabbing the towel below, he asked Veronica what was for breakfast. Then, as an afterthought he walked over to the stove and enveloped her in a hug from behind. He looked both ways to see if they were perhaps being watched and, deciding that the coast was indeed clear, nuzzled her neck while whispering in her ear.

"Do you know how happy you've made me, *frau*?"

"Careful, you," she warned. "Maybe we should save the *shmuzzling* for the bedroom? She's getting older, ya know."

"Yes, I know that. Makes no difference, does it?" he asked.

"Yes, it does, you," she answered sternly, swatting his arm with a hot pad. He feigned dejection but quickly changed the subject.

"What's for breakfast? Do I smell *kaffi* soup?" Henry asked, running his fingers through his hairs.

"Yes. With biscuits. You like that," she said turning around and hugging him back.

Not one to miss this opportunity, he kissed her gently and could tell right away that she'd wanted to kiss him too. He kissed her in earnest until she pulled away, catching her breath.

"Enough now, you," she said. "It can wait. On another note here, she asked me to tell her about her *mamm* again. I think she is *chust* trying to understand where she fits into all of this," Veronica ventured.

"I know," Henry said nodding. "I think we just answer what she asks, not much more till she's ready and asks again, sort of processing what she can handle at the time."

"I agree. I don't want it to be a big mystery either, but *chust* part of our story. And normal too. I think she can see how happy we are and how much she is loved and wanted. That's what every child needs. She isn't lacking there, I doubt," Veronica added.

"You're right, ya know. I've been thinking, too," Henry said as he took his seat at the head of the table. Veronica looked at him as she brought the bowls to the table, giving him leave to explain.

"There will always be things we need to figure out, but as long as we can keep the lines of communication open, we can tackle anything. I was so worried before we got married that I should have all the answers all the time. That was exhausting," he said, shaking his head.

"*Ach*! It sure was. I was ready to throw in the towel more than once for sure," Veronica remembered, shaking her head.

"I made it rather hard, I'm afraid, with all my speculating and pontificating. It could have been the end of us, ya know. But somehow you got the idea into your head to *kumm* all the way to Canada and straighten me out, eh?" Henry added.

"I still don't believe I did that. Pretty gutsy if you ask me. It worked though, eh? With Aunt Wanda all agreeing with me," she remembered as she took three mugs from the cupboard and set them on the table.

Just then Rose came skipping in, swinging the half-filled wire egg basket, still humming as the back door slammed with a thud. Her bare feet were covered with wet grass and her black *kapp* was already hanging down her back by its strings. Veronica stopped what she was doing to take in the toenails once again, incredulous at this child's imagination. *Not really all that different from how my own mind works, I guess,* she thought to herself. *Wait till Henry hears this one. Never a dull moment, eh?*

"The chicks haven't hatched yet but I left that one alone

so she wouldn't peck me," Rose reported. Then she tipped her head and stood still in the middle of the kitchen frowning.

"I chust want to know how the eggs get there. I mean who puts them under the chickens for me to find?" she puzzled aloud. Henry and Veronica burst out laughing at that. Henry had to take his bandana handkerchief out of his pocket and wiped his eyes, still laughing.

"*Sits ana*," Veronica said, finally collecting herself, and called Rose to the table. "Hurry and wash first. It'll get cold."

Acknowledgments

I have given birth to a series of books full of true stories and memories gathered from a lifetime of amazing encounters with other cultures and diverse peoples.

I owe a great debt to the mothers and babies I have had the privilege of serving for so many years and all I learned from each one: Amish *mamms*, Hutterite *mutters*, Hmong *nias*, Vietnamese, Somali, Ethiopian, Native American, and all the other brave women I have met.

I also owe a great debt of gratitude to WOW (Women of Words) and NLW/RWA (Northern Lights Writers/Minnesota chapter of Romance Writers of America) and Patricia Morris (past president of MIPA, Minnesota Independent Publishers Association,) and Phyllis Moore, all author-friends who have so unselfishly shared their wisdom and experience of the writing and publishing world with me. I couldn't have done this without each one of you!

And Janet Marchant, librarian, beta reader extraordinaire, and a dear friend, thanks for her advice, suggestions and expertise in all things books. Thank you!

I want to especially thank Nancy Schumacher and her brilliant team at Melange Books who were my midwives and doulas throughout the birthing of my books.

Special thanks goes to Sister Kristine Haugan, OCDH, who is one of my most supportive fans and beta reader. Nothing gets past you, does it?

Of course, I can't end without expressing my eternal

gratitude to my dearest husband of 48 years, David, and my children, Abraham, Isaac, Ruth, Rachel, and HRuthh Rose for their undying love, encouragement and support no matter how *ferhoodled* mother's latest creation appears to be.

THANK YOU FOR READING

Did you enjoy this book?

We invite you to leave a review at your favorite book site, such as Goodreads, Amazon, Barnes & Noble, etc.

DID YOU KNOW THAT LEAVING A REVIEW...

- Helps other readers find books they may enjoy.
- Gives you a chance to let your voice be heard.
- Gives authors recognition for their hard work.
- Doesn't have to be long. A sentence or two about why you liked the book will do.

About the Author

Midwife-turned-author, Stephanie Schwartz seems to swim seamlessly through cultures, religions, superstitions, raw fear and ecstasy to the first breath of a new baby. She knows how birth works and invites her readers to join her, taking us on a tour to the innermost workings of another world while giving us a rare, intimate glimpse into her daily life. She has five children scattered around the world, grandchildren, and over a thousand babies she calls her own. After writing three books on birth, (published under her married name, Sorensen) and then retiring as a midwife, began her foray into fiction. Thanks to the Pandemic she was able to produce the four novels in the Amish Nurse Series.

facebook.com/authorstephanieschwartz

newamishromance@yahoo.com

Also by Stephanie Schwartz

The Amish Nurse Series
Worry Ends Where Faith Begins
Time Will Tell
Playing on the Outhouse Roof
The Pearl of Great Price

The Amish Veronica Series
Wherever You Go There You Are
You Have Ravished My Heart
Merry Amish Christmas (Coming Soon!)

Made in the USA
Middletown, DE
05 February 2025